GW00854907

Muddle is My Middle Name

Kay Kinnear

Scripture Union

To our North Carolina companions of
The Real World:
Marilyn, Doyle, Sharon, Dave and their families

Copyright © 2001 Kay Kinnear
First published 2001

Scripture Union, 207–209 Queensway, Bletchley,
Milton Keynes, MK2 2EB, England.

ISBN 1 85999 457 1

All rights reserved. No part of this publication may be
reproduced, stored in a retrieval system, or transmitted in
any form or by any means, electronic, mechanical,
photocopying, recording or otherwise, without the prior
permission of Scripture Union.

The right of Kay Kinnear to be identified as author of this
work has been asserted by her in accordance with the
Copyright, Designs and Patents Act 1988.

British Library Cataloguing-in-Publication Data.
A catalogue record of this book is available from the British
Library.

Printed and bound in Great Britain by Creative Print and
Design (Wales) Ebbw Vale.

Chapter 1

"Take Mini Muddle with you," Mum called from upstairs.

"Oh, *Mum*, do I *have* to?"

"The cash'n'carry asked me to work this afternoon. We need the money, Lucy.

Lucy muttered under her breath, "We always need the money." With dad on short time at the engineering works, there never seemed enough to go round.

She shouted back, "Why can't Dad or Buddy look after Mini for once?"

Mum came clattering down the stairs. (The old stair carpet had been pitched out last year.) Her dark hair showed strands of grey and she looked tired. She said, "Dad's working on the car and your big brother's stacking shelves at the supermarket." She slung her bag over her shoulder. "Anyway, you're Mini's favourite."

Right on cue, Lucy's little brother roared round the corner of the lounge. He crashed his toy car into a table leg.

"Brrmmmm," he bellowed.

Of course, Mini Muddle or Mini wasn't his real name. He was Nicholas, and dad called him a chip off Lucy's block because Lucy was the *Big* Muddle of the family. Lucy Madeleine – she was always in a scrape. Whenever Buddy wished to be annoying (most of the time), he called her Lucy Muddle-on.

There was that time she tripped on the rumpled up rug and shot a scoop of double fudge ice cream into the air. It landed splat! in their neighbour's open handbag. Chocolate hairbrush, chocolate bus pass. Yummee!

There was the time she muddled her dad into taking the rubbish to Oxfam and their nicely washed old clothes to the dump; the time she shut Sophie's plaits in the door; the time she flooded the bathroom and – other times.

But now, Lucy had promised herself, Mini could take over as the family Muddle. Things were going to change. *She* was going to really, really, really concentrate on keeping out of trouble. She was going to Become Organised, so she could make her dream come true.

Her mum interrupted her thoughts. "Are you and Michelle going to Twin Oaks shopping centre?" Lucy nodded. "Would you get Mini's picture taken? There's a photo contest at Jameson's with £100 prize for the most photogenic child."

Lucy giggled, "Him!!?"

Mum laughed too as they considered his chances. His face was grubby, but he wasn't bad to look at. Like Lucy, he had short, curly brown hair that showed gold bits in the sun. He had Lucy's deep brown eyes and turned-up nose, too. Then he sneezed and the turned-up nose dripped goo.

"He won't win, of course," said Mum, scooping him up. She wiped his nose and gave him a hug.

"I want down," he said, waving his arm. Mum's glasses went flying.

"He's got your genes all right, Lucy," said Mum.

"No. My jeans are too big, ho, ho," said Lucy. She and her dad loved word jokes.

Mum groaned and picked up her spectacles. She explained about the contest. "They give you a free photo. We'll frame it and give it to Gran for her birthday."

"She'd like that," Lucy said.

"Right. So put him in his new navy-and-white knitted top, the one with the white collar. Take a damp face-flannel in a plastic bag. Clean him up before the photo. Keep an eye on him. Don't get distracted and forget about the contest."

"And have a nice day, Lucy," Lucy added.

"And have a nice day, Lucy," Mum grinned at Lucy. They were eye-level already. She'd be taller soon. "You're a good girl. If only..." her mum stopped.

"If only *what*?" asked Lucy. But she knew the answer. If only you weren't such a disaster merchant.

"Nothing," said Mum. "Bye for now." She hurried out of the front door.

An hour later, Lucy, Mini Muddle in his new top and best jeans, and Lucy's friend, Michelle, were standing at the bus-stop.

"Sorry, Shell, about *him*. I couldn't get out of it," Lucy apologised.

"No worries," said Michelle. "At least he doesn't whinge like Freddy." She pulled her baseball cap down over her face. Lucy guessed it was to shut out the horrible thought of *her* little brother.

The bus rumbled round the corner, and Lucy stuck out her hand. They sat at the back of the bus, and Michelle started to tell Lucy about her cousin's new mobile phone.

Out of the corner of her eye, Lucy saw Mini lean over and pick up something from the floor. He opened his mouth to put it in, whatever it was. Lucy caught his arm.

"Let's see, Mini." He opened his hand. It was an orange sweet, sticky with fluff.

"Yuck, nasty! You can't eat that." She threw it out of the bus window. "You've got to watch him every minute," she said to Michelle.

Mini turned round to stare out of the back window. "N'orange sweetie is losted," he said, sadly.

Lucy took the face-flannel out of her bum-bag and wiped his sticky hand. "Could you *please* stay clean till your photo's taken?"

The bus dropped them off at the corner by the sports store, Lucy's favourite shop. "Let's visit my trainers," she said.

Lucy's dream was to be a runner – an international sports star who travelled the world and signed autographs. She imagined herself at the Olympics, running a lap of honour, draped in a flag. Only sometimes she saw her legs getting tangled in the flag. How awful to fall flat in front of thousands of people! She shook her head to get rid of the thought.

She and Michelle pressed their noses to the sports shop window. Directly in front were the most gorgeous running shoes Lucy had ever seen. They had red and navy stripes on the side, thirty per cent extra cushioning, and waffle pattern soles for good grip. She'd been inside several times to ask all about them.

"Aren't they beautiful?" Lucy sighed.

"How much have you got saved?" asked Michelle.

"Just over £18."

"That's not even half," Michelle said.

"I know. Mum said I'd better get busy and pray. So I have."

"What good will that do?"

Lucy replied, "I believe God answers when you talk to him."

"What, *always*?" Michelle was amazed, Lucy could see.

"Well, Mum says sometimes the answers aren't what you were expecting. She says I should pray to be patient while I save. But I sort of just pray straight *for* my trainers."

Lucy grinned at Michelle. "Anyway, Dad's made me a promise. If I can save up £25 by my birthday, he'll put up the rest."

"Not long to go," said Michelle.

"I know. I do extra jobs at home and for our neighbour, Granny George. But everybody's short of cash right now."

She looked down at Mini Muddle. "Want to see my trainers?" She lifted him up to the window and pointed.

"Get them now?" he asked, patting her cheek.

"I wish," she said, and put him down.

They headed for the shopping centre. They spotted the photo queue long before they could see Jameson's department store. Children in party clothes stood with their parents in a line which snaked round to the town park. They joined the end of the queue.

"This could get boring," Michelle said.

"Want to see some training exercises Buddy showed me?" asked Lucy. Without waiting for an answer Lucy flung her arms up and jumped as high as she could. Then she dropped down in a squat and leapt up again four more times.

"Those are squat jumps," Lucy panted. "Leg exercises you do five times. Try." The parents queuing shuffled up to give them more room.

Michelle jumped up and down twice and stopped. "Why am I doing this?" she complained. "I want to be a nurse."

"Do arm exercises then," said Lucy. "You're pretty small. You'll need big muscles to lift all those wobbly sick people."

Michelle stuck out her tongue.

Mini bounced up and down too. Then he crawled up on to a low wall along the edge of the park. "See me, Lucy," he cried.

"Lovely," said Lucy. She gave him a glance and then started to demonstrate a step exercise.

Suddenly Mini Muddle shouted, "SKIRREL!"

Lucy whirled round. Her little brother was a long way up a tree. Above him a squirrel scolded noisily. Cheecheechee.

"SEE ME, LUCY," Mini shouted again. He looked pleased. His arms and legs just reached round the trunk.

"NICH-O-LAS!" Lucy screamed. "HANG ON, I'M COMING!"

Lucy jumped over the wall and raced toward the tree. Mini screwed his head round and looked down. Something about her face seemed to scare him. He started to slide, bumping back down the trunk. Just before he reached Lucy's arms, his head scraped past a broken-off twig.

"OW! OW!" he howled.

Lucy knelt with him in her arms.

"I hurted my head," Mini sobbed. He lifted his hand to show his wound, a small graze on his forehead. It was bleeding a little.

"Poor baby," Lucy said. She gave him a cuddle.

"I saw a skirrel," he said suddenly through his tears.

"Is he all right?" asked Michelle. "The lady behind us in the queue is saving our place."

"It's only a little cut and Mini is very brave," Lucy said, smiling at him.

She got out the flannel and sponged the scrape. Then she wiped his hands. A lady from the queue gave Lucy a plaster and she pasted it in place.

Then she noticed the front of his shirt. It was covered in mossy green streaks and brown splodges from the bark. Her heart sank.

"Maybe it'll wipe off," Michelle suggested. They both scrubbed at the front. But it was hopeless.

Lucy looked at her watch. "There's not time to go home for another shirt. What am I going to do?"

"He looks terrible." agreed Michelle. "Is there any point in staying?"

"I'll be in trouble – again – if I don't. Mum wants a photo for Gran's birthday," Lucy said.

"Maybe he could hold a toy in front of him or a book," suggested Michelle.

"Right. Called *How to Disappear Your Little Brother*." They giggled and Mini, who didn't realise he was the joke, giggled too. Lucy stared at him, thinking hard. "Maybe he could wear the top backwards. It might look odd, but at least it would be clean."

"Better leave it to the last minute to change Mr Mess," Michelle warned.

Lucy laughed and nodded. "Let's go and find our place."

The queue had moved on a long way and they were almost at the front. Michelle helped Lucy to take Mini's top off and turn it round. The back was plain navy and clean, so that was all right. "What about the plaster?" asked Michelle.

"Could he wear your baseball cap, Shell?"

Michelle plopped it on Mini's head. It fell down over his eyes. The little boy stood still. "Can't see," he said.

"Brilliant," Michelle said.

"We could turn it round." Lucy gave it a spin. With the peak at the back, at least his face could be seen.

They backed away to look at him critically. Lucy burst out laughing. "He looks like our vicar!" she cried. "It's the dark shirt and that thin white collar. It's backwards just like our vicar Mr Cole wears."

"Great," said Michelle. "A mini vicar in a baseball cap."

"It's hopeless," Lucy agreed. "But if he smiles nicely, that's all Gran will care about."

"Next!" called the photographer.

The photographer was an oldish man, forty maybe, with a droopy face. He looked surprised when he saw Mini Muddle. But he only said, "He's under five, isn't he?"

Lucy nodded. She put Mini in a raised chair in

front of the camera. "His name is Nicholas," she told the photographer.

The photographer fiddled with his camera for a minute. Then he called, "Look this way, Nicholas. Look at the teddy!" And he jiggled a small teddy bear in his hand.

Mini glanced up. He smiled a beautiful prize-winning smile. He loved teddies. But just as the camera flashed, he frowned and pointed at the bear.

"Teddy's got a sore eye," he told the photographer. Peering at the bear, Lucy saw one of its eyes was hanging loose.

"Pity about that," the photographer said. "Such a lovely smile the second before." He put the bear down. "Never mind, each child is allowed two free shots."

He nodded at Lucy. "Come and stand beside me. Call out his name when I tell you and mention something he likes." He refocused the lens and said, "OK" softly.

"Hey, Mini!" called Lucy. "Where's your dumper truck?"

His face lit up. Just as the flash went, he bounced in his chair and his cap shot forward over one eye. His lips puckered into a "brmmmm, brmmmm," shape.

"Awwwww," the photographer said, crossly. "Couldn't you have said, 'ice cream'?"

"He hates ice cream," Lucy returned, quick as a camera flash. It was nearly true. He hated rum and raisin.

The photographer sighed. "It'll be an unusual shot, anyway. You can console yourself with that." He handed Lucy two forms. "Fill out his name, address and age on this one and give it back to me. The other one's for ordering reprints and enlargements. You'll have to wait about half an hour for your picture. We've got behind."

"Can't you post it?" asked Lucy. She handed back the first form, filled in.

"All right," he said, scribbling "post pic" on Mini's form. Next!" he called. A little girl with blond curls and big blue eyes strutted in beside her mum.

Lucy, Michelle and Mini left the studio. "We could have waited," Michelle said.

Lucy's shoulders slumped. "I couldn't face it. I've really blown it. He was never going to win, but now there's no decent photo for Gran."

"It wasn't your fault," said Michelle.

"Mum won't see it that way. She'll think I was careless. As usual."

"I don't," said Mini. He looked worried.

"You don't what, monster?" asked Lucy.

"Hate ice cream," he said, his brown eyes wide.

Lucy grinned. He couldn't help it if he wasn't a prize-winner. "I'll remember that."

Lucy and Michelle decided to forget about the photo disaster. No point in spoiling the whole day. After a stroll round, they popped into a toy store. They played the new game Krazykool and Mini rode a little lorry. Then they wandered through the market and tried on baseball caps at their favourite stall.

Martha, the stallholder said, "How many years since you lot bought anything?"

Michelle said, "When we're rich and famous, we'll be your best customers."

"That'll be right," she said. But she gave them a friendly wave when they went to buy an ice cream. They put their money together. It would just stretch to three cornets.

"I like ice cream," Mini Muddle said, happily. Soon the lower half of his face was a chocolate smear.

On the way home they went back to the sports shop for one more goggle at Lucy's trainers. This time she noticed a sign:

SALE STARTS NEXT WEEK.

She popped her head through the door and asked the assistant, "Will those red and navy trainers at the front of the window be on sale?"

"Sorry, love," he said. "that's our most popular model. It's end-of-line stuff for our sale."

"Oh. Thanks." Lucy shut the door again. "I should be so lucky."

Then she told Michelle about a coach at Merlins' Athletics Club. "Buddy says he'll try to introduce me. If I show promise, they'll invite me to join Junior Merlins when I'm eleven! Only," Lucy added slowly, "I've got to have proper running shoes even for a trial."

"Keep saving," said Michelle.

It wasn't till later that Lucy began to worry again about Mini's picture. The right thing would be to tell Mum the truth straight out. Say he'd got dirty and fidgeted and the picture was ruined.

But Lucy's mum wasn't home when they got back. When she did come rushing in, carrying shopping, there was a fuss about Buddy going out clubbing. If there was a good moment to tell her mum, Lucy missed it.

In church on Sunday, Lucy started to pray for Mini's photo to be all right. But she knew it wouldn't be. She'd do better to ask God to help her to be brave and be honest with Mum. She closed her eyes and prayed silently.

On Monday, as Lucy hunted round for her PE kit, Mum mentioned the photo for the first time. "When did they say they'd send it?" she asked.

"They didn't say." Lucy took a deep breath. "Mum, about the photo..."

"I'm really looking forward to seeing it," Mum interrupted. "He's at such a sweet stage. Gran will love it."

Lucy gulped. Her mouth was dry. "Mum..." she tried again.

"Yes?" mum looked up.

Lucy's courage failed. "Got to go now," she said, swallowing hard. As she hurried out the door, she thought to herself – you chickened out, Lucy Lily-Liver. For shame!

Chapter 2

Every morning Lucy lurked near the front door hoping to catch the post before school. She had decided in the end to tear up the picture before Mum saw it. It wouldn't be a decent photo for Gran anyway. Lucy reasoned that when the photo didn't arrive her mum would think it had got lost in the post. With so many pictures from the contest, it would be easy for one to go missing. Lucy didn't feel exactly right about it, especially since Mum would be disappointed. But it hadn't really been Lucy's fault. Well, not entirely her fault. All right, it had been her fault, but she hadn't *meant* things to go wrong.

Six days passed. No photo. Lucy began to relax. Maybe it really had been lost in the post. Then on Saturday morning, she heard her mum cry out, "Lucy, come here! It's Mini Muddle's picture!"

Lucy's heart flipped. She had forgotten to get to the post first. Now she was for it. She trudged downstairs and into the lounge.

Something was wrong with Mum! She was dancing around waving a piece of paper. "He's won! He's won! He's won £75! Look at this!" The words tumbled out. "£75 for the most unusual photo!"

Lucy's jaw dropped. She stared at the figure 75

on the award notice. Then her mum thrust the photo in front of her eyes. There was Mini in his vicar's outfit, with the backwards baseball cap tilted over one eye. His hands were held up, as if to catch an invisible ball. His mouth was puckered, going "brmmmm." It was unusual all right.

Mum grabbed Lucy and gave her a bear hug. She babbled, "How clever of you to go for the prize where he'd have the best chance. I didn't even know there *was* a prize for an unusual picture. I can't have read the notice very carefully. Did you and Michelle dream up this outfit together?"

She studied the photo again and burst out laughing. "He does look a sight! You're a genius." She smiled at Lucy. "Genius, of course, merits a reward."

"Mum," Lucy gulped. "It was all a mistake. I let Mini get dirty. That's why his shirt's on backwards. I was afraid the picture would be spoiled and you'd be so cross. I should have told you."

"Yes, you should. You'll be easier in your mind if you deal honestly with people. And that includes your mum! It's what Christians always try to do. But in this case, Lucy, things have turned out better than a certain person deserves." She kissed Lucy's cheek. "Anyway, you can have your birthday trainers whenever you want."

"Brilliant!" Lucy did a squat jump for joy.

Mum went on, 'We'll have another picture taken for Gran's present. This one might be a little *too* unusual." She giggled. "There should even be money left for a little toy for our star."

At that moment, the star zoomed into the room and fell over the edge of the rug. The box in his hand exploded plastic bricks all over the lounge. Lucy jumped back and her foot skidded on a brick. She thumped down. "OOOOF!" Straight on to a plate of buttered toast on the coffee table.

"Oh, Mum, sorry!" Lucy stood up and twisted round to look at her buttery bottom.

"There goes breakfast," said Mum. But she was smiling.

Lucy swung a plastic shopping bag and whistled, 'What a Wonderful World'. It was a pop song about a million years old. Dad was always singing it in a terrible gravelly voice. For once, though, it was just how she felt. She gave the bag a full-circle swing. Inside the bag was a box. Inside the box were trainers with red and navy stripes! At last!

Buddy had come with her to the shop, to make sure she was getting the best sort for running. Miracle of miracles, he had agreed with her choice. She'd wanted to wear them straight away, naturally. But he'd said she should go for a run in her old trainers. Feet expand when they're hot. Then she should try on the new ones to make sure they were big enough. He could be a right pain. But she wanted to stay in his good books, so he'd talk to that coach.

Buddy had gone on to work. So all she had to do was buy toothpaste at the chemist for Mum and then she could go home and test out her trainers.

Ten minutes later Lucy was standing at the Number 23 bus stop. The only other person waiting was an old lady with snow-white hair and a yellow daffodil pinned to her blue coat. Two bags of shopping sat propped against the bus stop post.

"I like your flower," Lucy said.

The old lady smiled and her bright blue eyes crinkled up. "I always feel happy when the first daffs come. Spring is here." She touched the flower. "I've been to church to arrange flowers for tomorrow's service. But I thought the Lord wouldn't mind if I wore one myself."

"I go to church too," Lucy said. "Which church is yours?"

The old lady pointed. "It's the small red brick one over there."

"Mine's the one with the tall spire on St. John Street."

The old lady nodded. "I went there to the carol service at Christmas. Really lovely!"

"Our youth group sang 'Shepherds' Rocking Carol' with a guitar," Lucy said. She sang the first line – 'Hush you, Jesus, baby King.'

"I remember it," said the old lady. "Oh look, here's the bus." She stooped slowly to pick up her shopping. As she lifted it, one of the bags broke open. Cans and packets and bits fell all over the pavement.

"Oh dear," said the old lady. Hanging on to the bus stop post, she began to bend down.

"Hurry up," called the bus driver. He frowned. "Can't wait all day. I'm already 12 minutes behind schedule."

"Sorry," she panted. "I'm a bit stiff. I've got arthritis."

"I'll help," Lucy said. She stuffed her mum's toothpaste into her pocket and took her trainers box out of the carrier bag. Quickly she began to put the dropped food into the bag. A can of potatoes went rolling down the hill. She chased after it and snatched it up just at the kerb. Waving the can, she jogged back to the bus stop. "You almost had mashed potatoes!" she said.

The old lady giggled. She sounded surprisingly young. "I *like* mashed potatoes, but not with tyre marks."

The bus had gone.

"He wouldn't wait," the old lady said. "Thank you for your help. I'm so sorry I've made you miss your bus."

"No problem," said Lucy.

The old lady smiled. "You're quick on your feet, I noticed."

"I want to be a runner." Lucy opened her box. "These are my new trainers, my first proper running shoes. Aren't they beautiful!"

The next bus didn't come for a while. The old lady was pretty clued up on athletics, Lucy was amazed to find. She wanted to know whether Lucy was going to be a sprinter, a middle-distance or long-distance runner. Lucy explained she was too young to decide. But her brother thought she was going to be too tall for the long-distance.

When they finally boarded a bus, it was crowded. A boy gave up his seat to the old lady and Lucy stood for a while. Then she sat at the back.

Two stops from home, Lucy spotted Michelle waiting at the traffic-lights. Lucy pressed the bell, said a quick "Bye-nice-meeting-you" as she passed the old lady and hopped off the bus.

"Hey, Shell! Saw you from the bus," Lucy jogged to catch up with her friend. "Want to come over? I've got something brilliant to show you."

Then she looked down at her hands. They were empty. She'd left her brand-new trainers on the bus! And the Number 23 had disappeared round the corner.

The worst thing in the world had happened.

Chapter 3

"Don't cry, love," Mum said.

Lucy buried her head in her arms. Her shoulders shook. "I'm stupid and useless and careless and muddly –" Lost for any more hideous words, Lucy simply sobbed.

Mum handed her a tissue and ruffled her hair. "Dry your eyes and blow your nose. I'll make you some cocoa, and then we'll see what we can do."

Lucy drank the hot, sweet drink while Mum phoned the bus garage. She described the trainers and their box, gave the time they were left and the bus number. Then she waited and waited for the lost property officer to check. Finally she spoke again.

Lucy held her breath.

"Thanks anyway," Mum said, and gave her name and phone number in case the trainers turned up later.

Lucy slumped.

Then Mum phoned the police and went through it all again.

"Nothing so far, Lucy," Mum said. She put her arm round Lucy's shoulder. "I'm so sorry. It's very hard to lose something so precious. But you do rush at life and don't stop to think."

"I *know*," Lucy wailed. "And I *planned* to be

better.

Mum asked, "Shall we pray about it together?" Lucy's "yes" was almost a whisper. She and Mum held hands and closed thier eyes.

"Dear Lord," prayed Mum, "if it is your will please help Lucy to get back her trainers. This loss is making her very sad. But give her the strength to bear up and be cheerful whatever happens. Help our much-loved girl to conquer this failing that gives her – and the rest of her family too sometimes – so much trouble. We ask this in Jesus' name. Amen."

"Amen," breathed Lucy.

Dad and Buddy came home. Everybody gave her a hug, even Mini Muddle. Nobody, not even Buddy, said it served her right for being such an airhead.

When Lucy could trust herself not to cry again, she phoned Michelle to tell her 'no luck'. Then she played with Mini and read him a story. She helped Mum wash up after tea.

At eight o'clock the phone rang.

Dad answered. He soon gave Lucy a thumbs-up. "There's a lady on the phone who says she's got your trainers!"

Lucy started to jump up and down.

"It's a Mrs Moffat. She says she knows you. She met you at a bus stop."

Lucy went to the phone. Mrs Moffat said, "Right after you got off the bus, someone found your trainers. I thought I could locate you, so I took them. I phoned your church office, and left a message on the answerphone. They've just phoned back. I described you and how you want to be a runner."

Mrs Moffat laughed. "They knew right away who it was."

Then she spoke to Dad again and he was smiling as he listened.

When he hung up, he said, 'Listen to this, everybody. Mrs Moffat said she was very glad to return a favour to someone who'd helped her. She congratulated me on having such a polite, kind daughter."

Buddy snorted. "Lucky I didn't answer the phone. I'd have told her she'd got the wrong number – there was nobody here like that."

Lucy tried to poke him in the ribs, but he dodged out of reach. Grinning, he asked, "Want to go for a run in the park tomorrow afternoon?"

Lucy put on her new trainers. She and Dad had picked them up last night, after the phone call, and Lucy had slept with them beside her bed. This morning before church, she'd made her test run. The fit was perfect.

"Hurry up, Lucy," Buddy shouted from the front door. "I've got athletics training at half-past three. Don't forget to double-knot your laces."

Typical, Lucy thought. He hurried you up and then told you to do something. She jumped up. She'd double-knot them when they got to the park.

It had rained the night before. The air was fresh and the trees were starting to turn green. Only two streets away, their local park wasn't large, but it had a wilderness bit by the railway line and a path all round the tidy part. This circuit, plus some crossing tracks, meant a decent run was possible.

One path circled a pond with an island, where ducks and geese nested.

After warm-up exercises, Buddy and Lucy set off, one jogging, one running, so they could stay side by side. All at once, Buddy stretched out his long legs and raced ahead down one of the crossing paths. He stopped and turned to watch Lucy run. When she caught up, he said, "You've got a nice, easy lope. Now try lengthening your stride. Push the ground away as you run. Try it for a short distance."

"OK," Lucy said. She'd show him. She began to run hard, reaching out each stride as far as she could. Wow! She was really motoring. Maybe sprinting would be her thing after all.

Suddenly, there was a sharp tug on her foot and she plunged forward. THUD! She landed on the muddy edge of the path. She sat up and rubbed her hand. Mud slurped down her right track suit leg, At the end of the leg was a trainer with untied laces. She'd forgotten the double knots. Lucy sighed and shut her eyes.

When she opened them, Buddy was standing over her, staring at the trailing laces. His dark eyes looked black under his thick eyebrows. His mouth was set in a straight line. He shook his head. But all he said was, "Let's go to the pond and mop you off, Lucy Muddle-on."

The bank was raised and rocky on one side. Buddy gave her the red bandanna he used as a sweatband, and she leaned over to wet it. She rubbed away at the mud, not very successfully. As she leaned forward for more clean water, she heard a rustle in the bushes along the bank. Probably a bird. Maybe a rat. Lucy shivered and inched away.

Then there was a peep and a fluffy brown duckling came out from under the leaves.

"Buddy, look, a baby duck!" Lucy cried. She gazed all round. "Where's its mum?"

Buddy knelt further along the pond and held up brown and tan feathers. Lucy saw some scattered fluffy bits. "What's happened?"

"Maybe a fox came up the rail line and took a duck family. They might have been out of the water, feeding on bits of bread."

"That's terrible!" wailed Lucy.

"Terrible for the duck family, but the fox might be a mum feeding her own cubs."

"We can't leave it here all by itself. A dog or another fox will get it. Can we take it home?"

"Lucy, you know Dad's allergic to animal hair."

"This isn't hair – it's feathers. Fluff."

Buddy shrugged. "I don't really know about feathers. It might be all right."

Lucy picked up the duckling and stroked its soft head. "Oh, he's so sweet." She zipped him into her bum-bag, just leaving his head sticking out. He didn't struggle.

They walked home, not wanting to jolt the baby duck by jogging. Buddy collected his sports kitbag from the front hall and said to Lucy, "See you later. Good luck with the duck."

Lucy tiptoed up to the bedroom she shared with Mini Muddle. She put crumpled newspaper into her trainer box and an old pair of knickers on top. Then she punched holes all over the lid.

When she put the duckling inside, she told him, "I'm going to look for food and water. Back soon."

She replaced the lid and slid the box under her bed.

In the kitchen she grated some brown bread into crumbs. She took a jam jar lid for water and found a piece of wilted parsley in the fridge. It *looked* like pondweed. Maybe the little duck wouldn't know the difference.

He did, though. He ignored the parsley, but ate crumbs from her hand. She poured a little water into his beak, then settled him on to the soft cloth and closed the lid.

Downstairs in the lounge, she looked outside. Mum and Mini were in the back garden, planting something. Great! Plenty of time to check out ducks in Dad's book on allergies and their treatments.

No ducks were listed in the index. Birds were, though. She sat down to read. The sentences were so complicated she couldn't tell whether birds gave problems or not. Why didn't adults just say what they meant, straight out?

"What are you reading with such interest?" asked Mum. She was carrying a trowel. Lucy hadn't heard her come in.

"I thought you were out planting," said Lucy, not answering the question.

"We are. I've come in for a big spoon so Mini can dig too." She went back outside.

Lucy read a bit more, but couldn't decide about the duck. She'd ask Buddy to read it tonight, but keep the duck hidden till then.

An hour later, Lucy came down to the kitchen for a snack.

Mum was making Mini a mini-sandwich. 'Why were you reading Dad's allergy book?" she asked.

Drat! She'd forgotten to put the book back on the shelf. "Oh, er, a girl at school has problems and I was wondering about it."

Mum looked closely at Lucy. Lucy didn't meet her eyes.

Just then they heard a yell. "Mummy! Mummy!"

Standing at the top of the stairs was a beaming Mini. "Mummy, I found a birdie!"

Chapter 4

Mum, Mini and Lucy sat at the kitchen table. In the middle of the table was Lucy's trainer box and the duck.

He looked out. "Peep!" he said. He turned his head and seemed to be sizing up the family.

Dad was leaning against the counter, keeping his distance. He was tall and slim like Buddy and Lucy. The only titch in the family was Mum.

"Rescuing an abandoned duck isn't terrible," Mum said, looking at Dad, "but Lucy knows about your allergies and she didn't tell me the truth."

"There *is* a girl at school with asthma!" Lucy cried. Then her face fell. She did normally try to tell the whole truth. "But that wasn't why I had the book out," she admitted.

"Exactly!" declared Mum.

"Don't be too hard on her." Dad held out an arm and Lucy went to stand with him. She could tell he was on her side. "She wanted to find out first whether a duck would give me trouble, so she could build a case for keeping it. Am I right?"

Lucy nodded.

"How about this for a plan?" Dad said. 'The duck stays in Lucy's and Mini's room for just a few weeks. When he's bigger, he goes outside to the back porch. Then, when he's grown enough to look after himself, we'll take him back to the park pond."

"Oh, *Dad.*"

"Lucy, the duck's a mallard. He's one of God's *wild* creatures in this beautiful world of ours."

Buddy and Lucy, and even Mum, started to whistle, 'What a Wonderful World', Dad's funny old song.

Dad laughed, "All right, you lot. Anyway he doesn't deserve a life of captivity."

"Keep the ducky?" asked Mini, who hadn't followed the discussion.

Dad swung Mini up to sit on his shoulder. "What shall we name him? Better be a unisex name. We don't know if it *is* a him."

Buddy said, "Let's call him Roast Duck."

"Horrible!" cried Lucy.

"Duck Soup?"

Dad informed Buddy that names were a serious matter. He glanced up at Mini. "What shall we call the duck?"

"Truck?" suggested Mini.

"He's got a one-track-mind," said Dad.

"Don't you mean a one-truck mind?" asked Lucy.

Dad gave her a thumbs up. The rest of the family groaned.

Lucy picked up the duckling and stroked his soft head. "What shall we call you?" she asked softly.

He opened his little beak, "Peep!"

"Oh yes! Let's call him Peep!" Lucy cried. Everybody agreed, especially Peep.

Several days later, Lucy whizzed through getting

ready for school. With half an hour to spare, she could start teaching Peep to swim. Dad had said that ducks learn to swim by following their mums. And Lucy was the only mum he had.

Dad and Buddy, who were working early shifts this week, were already out of the bathroom and gone. Lucy set Peep in the basin while she ran the bath. She dropped in Mini's yellow rubber duck. It was too small and the wrong colour to be Peep's brown mum. But maybe he wouldn't remember that.

Placing Peep in the soap dish, she towed the rubber duck along the water by its beak. "See, that's how to do it."

"Peep," said Peep. She imagined he looked nervous. And very small in the soap dish.

Lucy perched on the edge of the bath and lowered him gently into the water. She pulled the rubber duck along in front of him. He didn't move. She tried again and gave him a gentle shove from behind. All of a sudden, his little webbed feet began to paddle. He paddled right behind the duck, all round the bath.

"Bravo!" cried Lucy. "Clever Ducky Peep! It took me weeks and weeks to learn to swim."

He paddled and paddled. It wasn't a smooth glide like big ducks. His feet were too small and the stroke too short.

"You need to lengthen your stride," Lucy told him. "Push the water away as you swim. Try it for a short distance." She giggled. "And, by the way, double-knot your laces."

All of a sudden, he dived. Only his stub of a tail stuck out of the water. Lucy held her breath, but he didn't tip back up. She panicked. Maybe he didn't know how to come up.

"Peep!" she called, and reached over to him on the far side of the bath tub. Then she lost her balance.

YIPES! Arms and legs waving wildly, she splashed down into the water. She gasped and spluttered and finally clambered back out of the tub. Where was Peep? There! Paddling happily near the plug end, he'd come up on his own. What a noodle she was! Even *she* should have known that a duck, titchy or not, wouldn't drown.

Her school uniform was sopping wet. She checked her watch on the shelf. It was late, past time to leave for school.

Lucy stripped off her clothes and hung them, dripping, over the towel rails. Thank goodness she hadn't been wearing her shoes. She pulled the plug and scooped up Peep. His little feet kept paddling till she wrapped herself and him in a towel.

She dashed for the bedroom. There, her dad had rigged up a combination cage and box for Peep. She kissed his head and popped him back in his home.

She'd got another blouse and cardigan, but what was she going to do for a skirt?

Mum had a new navy skirt. Maybe she could borrow it.

"MUM!" She bellowed down the stairs. No answer. "MUM!" still no answer.

She peered out of the back window. Mum and Mini were hanging clothes on the line at the far end of the garden. She banged on the window, but they couldn't hear. The window's lock was stiff and she couldn't open it.

She needed to go. It would probably be all right. She'd just borrow the skirt.

The only problem was, it was an ankle-length skirt. When she tried it on, she looked like somebody's granny. She rolled over the waistband a couple of times. OK, that would do.

She was late now, so she stuck her school shoes into her bag and put on her trainers. She'd run to school.

Ten minutes later, Lucy was just pelting round the corner of Bremner School when she heard RRRRRRRIP! She stared down in horror. She'd stepped on the hem and torn the skirt at the bottom. The waistband had been rolling down as she ran. She'd catch it from her class and her mum would kill her!

Another blooming muddle for Lucy Muddle-on.

She trudged sadly into school.

"LUCY, WHENEVER ARE YOU GOING TO LEARN TO BE MORE CAREFUL?"

It was after school. Mum was red in the face and spitting nails.

"You leave the bathroom half-flooded with mess and dripping clothes. Not to mention a duck dropping in the soap dish. Then—" Mum took a deep breath and started again. "THEN, WITHOUT PERMISSION, you take and ruin my brand-new skirt." She threw up her hands. 'I get new clothes once in a blue moon and look what happens!!!

Lucy hung her head. And waited. There would be more.

"Nobody expects perfection from somebody your age. But Lucy, you do create more mess and muddle than anyone should expect. Stop and think. ONE, just before school is not a good time for swimming lessons. TWO, ask before you take. You could have had an *old* skirt of mine. THREE, if you borrow something special, handle it with extra care."

Still hanging her head, Lucy apologised. "I'm so sorry, Mum. I didn't mean it all to go wrong. I really will try harder."

Then she thought of something. "But I did teach Peep to swim!"

Mum gave a loud snort. Lucy looked up quickly. Mum was laughing. "Oh Lucy," she said, "whatever will we do with you?"

Surprisingly, a whole week passed before Lucy was in trouble again.

Chapter 5

Lucy lay in bed trying to feel ill and practising what to say. "Mum, I'm not feeling very well. I'd probably better stay at home today."

Hah! Her mum would pounce on that. *Where* don't you feel well? Tell me about it. Is it here, is it here? She'd be feeling Lucy's forehead, pressing her tummy, getting out the thermometer. Mum was on to every wobbly excuse to bunk off school.

Come to think of it, she *didn't* feel right at all. Butterflies were dancing in her stomach and her chest was tight. Lucy squeezed her eyes shut. She re-ran in her head yesterday's scene when Fitzie and Alice and the rest of their gang had blocked her way out of school ...

"Spaghetti-Legs, we've got a little outing planned for you tomorrow," Fitzie said, with a horrible grin. Fitzie (short for Sarah Fitzgerald) was Lucy's enemy. "I fancy a Kitkat about four o'clock and you're going to get it for me."

"You'll be lucky," Lucy said. "No more pocket money till Friday. Anyway, since when do I buy *you* goodies?"

"Who said anything about BUY?" Fitzie turned to Alice, "What did we enjoy last week, thanks to Collins Corner Shop? Tell her."

Alice counted off on her fingers. 'Two Toffee

Crisps. A Bounty. Three lollipops."

"And a pack of gum," chorused Sophie and Varsha, always willing to join in.

"Don't forget the ice lolly," added Marcie. She was new in the class and had just hooked on to this gang.

"That was a hard one, right out of the freezer, under their noses," Fitzie gloated. 'But we'll give you an *e-e-easy* target. Kitkats are just on the corner rack. Piece of cake. OK. Lucy?"

Lucy swallowed. "Do you mean you're pinching stuff?"

"Quick, isn't she?" Alice smirked.

"So, see you tomorrow, Spaghetti-Legs, *right here*," Fitzie said, pointing at the school gate.

Lucy wiped clammy hands down the side of her school skirt. She tried to keep her voice firm.

"N-no, I'm not going to do it. Why should I? The Collinses are nice. Anyway," she cleared her throat, "it's wrong to steal."

"Oh, listen to Goody Two-Shoes," sneered Alice.

Fitzie said, "You'll do it. Otherwise, you'll become a non-person. It'll be like you're *invisible*."

Alice laughed nastily. "You won't like that, especially with Michelle away. We have more plans for you, too, if you don't do what we say. See you *tomorrow*."

Then the five of them ran out of the gate sniggering, looking back over their shoulders and pointing at her...

Last night when she couldn't get to sleep, Lucy had talked over her problem with God. She'd asked him to help her stand against the gang. And be strong. She'd felt better afterwards and had finally dropped off.

But now that Alice's threatening *'tomorrow'* was today, Lucy felt afraid again. She rolled out of bed and wished she'd been more careful. Why hadn't she just said she had to go straight home after school. Why did she have to go all holy and pop out with, "It's wrong to steal." That had really put Alice's back up!

Malice Alice was what Michelle called her. Not to her face, naturally. Fitzie was bigger and tougher than anybody else in the class, but Alice was the one to worry about.

She was little and scary. Sort of pointed all over, pointy nose, pointy teeth, pointy elbows that dug into your ribs. Worst of all, a pointy mind that went straight to whatever would give you trouble.

Alice and Fitzie together were a force. They would see to it that *nobody at all* would talk to her for days.

Lucy sighed. She really didn't feel very well. Still in her pyjamas, she shuffled into the kitchen. Mini Muddle was finger-painting his egg and Mum was drinking tea.

Lucy tried out her excuse. "Um, Mum, I'm not feeling very well. I'd better stay at home today."

Mum shot her a glance and Lucy braced herself for questions. But all she said was, "I'm taking Mini to the doctor this morning for a checkup. He can look you over as well, if you're poorly."

"Go-ing doc-tor," sang Mini. He rubbed his nose with egg.

"Maybe, er–" Lucy stuttered, her mind racing. "maybe I'm just hungry. I couldn't eat that stuff with Brussels sprouts last night." She shivered.

"Brussels sprouts must be the worst food in the universe. Anybody would feel sick."

"That could be it," said Mum. Lucy looked at her suspiciously. Was that a tiny smile round her mouth?

Even with butterflies, Lucy was surprised to find she could put down an egg, coco crisps, and brown toast.

Then she set off for school.

The day was a nightmare waiting to happen. Fitzie and Alice and the rest were sweet as Creme Eggs all day. So sweet it made Lucy nervous. When she dropped her pencil during maths, Alice jumped up to get it.

"Here's your pencil, Lucy, *darling*." She smiled as if a Kitkat wouldn't melt in her mouth.

Varsha offered her a pocket dictionary during English. Fitzie handed her an apple at break. The gang saved a space at their table during lunch. Lucy couldn't refuse because all the girls' tables were full. She really would lose face if she went to sit with the boys.

As the day wore on, Lucy felt more and more jumpy. Why couldn't they just leave her alone? What had she ever done to them, apart from beat Fitzie in every race at last year's sports day. Maybe she could steal just the *one* Kitkat and then they'd leave her alone.

She wiped the back of her hand across her forehead. It felt sticky. Why did she never remember to bring a tissue? If only Michelle hadn't gone away. Where had she gone? Why was she away so long? She and Michelle were their own little gang. Everything was different when you had your best mate.

At three o'clock their teacher, Miss Morne (Miss Moan or Moany, she was known as) asked for a volunteer to water her plants after class. Miss Moan was big on green stuff. Their room had loads of pots scattered about, hanging spidery things and prickly cacti and geraniums, mostly with no flowers. Watering the plants was a long job. Lucy's hand shot up.

Miss Moan looked round the room for another hand. Lucy gazed round too. She remembered the last time she'd been watering monitor. She'd jumped down from the stool after doing a hanging plant, and the water had just whooshed out and down Moany's leg. Right into her shoe. Her screech had been awesome. Lucy tried not to giggle at the memory. It had been an accident, after all.

Miss Moan sighed. Lucy's hand was the only one waving in the air. "All right, Lucy, if you'll be very careful."

"Yes, Miss Morne."

At once, Lucy felt Alice's sharp elbow in her side. "Don't worry. We'll wait," she muttered.

Even watering one drop at a time, Lucy could make end-plant-thirst last only 20 minutes.

Finally, Miss Moan moaned, "Goodness! There's such a thing as being *too* careful, Lucy. Something I must say I never expected to say to you." She handed Lucy her homework book. "Thank you, be off home now."

Lucy tiptoed out of the school door and looked all around. Nobody. She sighed with relief. They'd got fed up with waiting. She slung her bag over her shoulder and hurried out of the gate.

"SURPRISE!" shouted five voices.

Lucy jumped like a kangaroo on hot coals as Fitzie's big hand grabbed her wrist. "I'm dying for my Kitkat. You must have watered the whole school." she said.

"Did you really think we wouldn't wait?" Marcie asked.

Lucy wrenched her arm from Fitzie's grip. Her mind was suddenly made up. "I'm not doing it."

Chapter 6

Fitzie's broad freckly face was close to Lucy's. She said, "Come on, just a little Kitkat, worth hardly anything. Collins will never miss it." Lucy stared into Fitzie's eyes. She thought they almost had a pleading look.

"What makes you so *good*?" Alice demanded. She made the word 'good' seem like 'slimy'.

Sophie piped up, "I know! She goes to that church across the street from my house. I see her sometimes on Sundays."

Four pairs of eyes focused on Lucy. Marcie must be acting as lookout because she had turned away and was gazing up the street.

"I get it!" said Alice, snapping her fingers. "She thinks she won't go to heaven if she nicks a Kitkat."

In spite of her fear, Lucy snorted. A rush of anger filled her chest and gave her courage. This lot were really brainless.

She said, "If you think believing in God is small and-and *stupid* like that, you're even thicker than I thought!"

"LET ME BY!" she shouted suddenly. Taking Fitzie by surprise, she shouldered her way past. Then she began to run. With a head start, even Fitzie hadn't a hope of catching Spaghetti-Legs.

It was a little victory, but it was followed by three days of misery. Nobody in the class spoke to her. Nobody at all. What was worse, the gang talked *about* her as if she weren't there.

"Do you remember that creep called Lucy? The funny looking one with Spaghetti-Legs and Pizza-Feet. Ho, ho. The goody-goody one, right? Whatever happened to her?"

Twice, when Miss Moan turned her back, Alice sat down – hard – on Lucy, as if the chair was empty.

The word that she was poison had gone down even to Class 5 where she had some friends. When the gang wasn't looking, Lucy thought she saw sympathetic glances. But nobody, not even the boys, wanted to get involved with big Fitzie and Malice Alice.

A non-person is exactly what Lucy felt like.

On Friday, after three long days of total freeze, Lucy felt shattered. Instead of her usual sprint home, she trudged slowly up and over the hill. Dumping her schoolbag in the hall, she dragged herself into the kitchen to make a cup of tea and a marmite sandwich.

Her mum glanced up from chopping carrots. "All right, Lucy Madeleine, what's the matter? Lately, you've been looking lower than a worm's back-side."

"Nothing." If she told Mum, she'd be down to school like a rocket. She could just hear the gang chanting: "Poor little mummy's gir-rl. Nobody's talking to her-rr." She'd never live it down.

"I'm missing Michelle. I wish she hadn't gone away." Oh how she wished she hadn't gone away.

"She's not your only friend, is she?" Her mother was definitely looking worried.

"No, but—"

"But what?" She laid down the carrot knife and put an arm around Lucy's shoulders. "What is it?"

The whole story came flooding out. It took some telling and a few tears.

"Well," her mum said, "we've got two things to deal with here. The shoplifting and the silent treatment." She shook her head in wonder and asked, "Are the boys also part of this no-talking business?"

"Yes." Lucy sniffed, "Even if they weren't, boys don't say anything worth listening to."

Suddenly, a long arm shot out and swept Lucy backwards. It pinned her to the kitchen wall and another hand covered her mouth.

"Take it back about boys," demanded Buddy with a huge grin. Coming into the kitchen, he must have heard her last sentence.

"–ully!" Lucy's voice was muffled.

"This isn't the time—" began Mum.

"Take it back."

"Won't." A choked-back giggle.

"I'll give you a big slobbery kiss." Buddy took his hand off Lucy's mouth.

"YUCKKK! I give in. Mum, make Buddy be nice to me; no one else is."

"Why is no one nice to you" asked Buddy, 'when you're so loveable?"

Lucy reached out to tweak his ear, but he fended her off.

"Stop it, you two," said Mum.

Then, for the second time, Lucy told her story.

Afterwards, her mum squared her shoulders as if she'd made a decision. "I'm going straight down to school on Monday and speak to your teacher and the head teacher."

"Oh Mummmmm! Please don't," Lucy wailed. "It's my word against five. Nobody else knows. The gang will say I'm making it up about the shoplifting. They'll tell the head teacher I'm being spiteful." She had to convince her. "And nobody EVER – EVER will speak to me again. Please, Mum."

Buddy patted Lucy on the head in a big-brother, maddening way, but he looked serious, "Mum, give her a little more time. Let her sort it herself if she can. She's done the right thing so far – stood up to pressure, spoken up for what she believes." He paused and Lucy noticed he put on an amazed voice, "Who'd have thought, Mum, that your and Dad's good Christian training would take hold in such a muddled head!"

Lucy tried to punch him, but he ducked out of her reach. Really, Lucy thought, he was the limit! Gives you a compliment, then takes it away with the next breath. Still, he seemed to be on her side.

"Lucy, I'm very much in two minds about this," said Mum, "but I'll give it a couple more days to see if it blows over. But the Collinses must be told."

Lucy quickly offered, "I'll pop into the shop after school on Monday and warn them."

Her mum hesitated. "All right. Buddy, can you meet Lucy there? She should have some back-up support. I'd come but I'm working." She turned to Lucy, "When's Michelle back?"

"Next week sometime. I hope Monday." Fingers crossed.

"OK, I'll wait till she's back and then give the head teacher a ring and tell her that some of her schoolchildren – no names – have been shoplifting. It wouldn't be right for us to let stealing go on and not do something about it. I'm sure she'll discuss it in assembly. If not, we'll think again."

"Oh, thanks, Mum." Lucy breathed a great sigh of relief. Come back soon, Michelle.

Michelle wasn't back on Monday. Lucy paced up and down at the corner of the playground by the sycamore tree, the place where they always met. Even after the bell she lingered, peering in the direction of Michelle's house. No sign of her best friend. Lucy thought Michelle could have visited thousands of cousins by now or whatever it was she was doing. She'd been really vague about her family's plans. It was odd. It wasn't like her to miss so much school. She'd have piles of lessons to copy up – and there was nothing she hated more.

So, another day with the wall of silence.

But, after all, things weren't so bad. Nobody talked to her, but they didn't rabbit on about her, or sit on her as if she'd disappeared. Maybe even Malice Alice had got bored with it.

Unless the gang was hatching up something new and grisly for her after school?

Chapter 7

Lucy had seen the five horrors giggling in the corner of the canteen. Would they all be lurking outside the school gate, ready to pounce? Well, she wouldn't wait for them to find her all alone. She'd rush out with the crush as soon as the bell went, scorch up the hill and be home before they could say boo.

Then she remembered. She had to go to Collins Corner Shop. Maybe she could run up one street toward home, circle round and reach the store by the back way. That might work.

When the bell went, she leapt out of her seat, grabbed her jacket and raced down the stairs. In a flash she was out of the door and off in the direction of home. She'd caught the gang off guard! Five minutes later, she was standing in front of Collins Corner Shop, not even out of breath.

Now, what to say? Should she tell it straight out? "Hi, Mrs Collins. Kids from school are pinching stuff from your store." Suppose nice Mrs Collins keeled over from the shock? She was really old, must be fifty at least. No, it should be more tactful like adults would say. "Good afternoon, Mrs Collins. Me and my mum think you should be made aware (that was good) that a few children are occasionally stealing items from your – er – premises." Yes, that was much better.

Trouble is, she hadn't remembered that so many kids would be pouring into those premises right after school. No sign of the gang, though, thank goodness. No sign of Buddy either. Maybe he'd be here by the time things quieted down. Meanwhile she could look for stationery and a card for Mother's Day.

Cards, paper, pens and pencils were at the back of the shop near the post office. The schoolkids stayed round the sweets near the front. Lucy set her schoolbag on the floor and started to look at cards. From the top row, she took down a huge card with a pink, padded satin heart and a gold 'To My Mother" surrounded by flowers. That would be a stunner for Mum. When Lucy looked at the back, it was a stunner price too. A smaller card would have to do. Why were they all so soppy?

My mum means all the world to me,
My ears thrill to her voice.
Today's her day, so let it be
That all our hearts rejoice.

Lucy doubted she would ever thrill to the sound of Mum's 'Your room looks like a hurricane hit it. I want it tidy before bedtime." Anyway, maybe she and Mini Muddle could make a card. Mum always loved home-made ones, even that time Lucy's card was so gluey Mum couldn't get it out of the envelope. Lucy began to look at stationery. There was blue, grey, pink, cream and yellow. There was a little pack of flower notelets reduced to under a pound. Or a small box of cream-coloured paper with a frilly edge.

Lucy checked the prices again and counted out her coins. She would have to hang on till Friday, when she got her next pocket money. She glanced up and noticed Ryan from her class waiting in the queue for the post office. Was she imagining it or was he giving her a very, very strange look? Had she got smuts on her nose, or what? She didn't know him very well. He mostly kept to himself. She lifted her hand in a half-wave and turned to go to the till.

Mrs Collins was taking money from the last school customer, a ginger-haired Infants boy with his mum. Still no Buddy. Lucy hurried forward.

"Hi, Mrs Collins," she began. Now, what was the rest? "Me and my mum thought uh – er, that is, some kids—" This was harder than she'd thought it'd be.

"Is there something special you wanted?" asked Mrs Collins, looking a little puzzled.

"Some kids—" Suddenly somebody moved on the other side of the front window behind Mrs Collins. A face smirked at her between the giant Easter eggs and the paper daffodils. Fitzie!

Lucy gulped and rushed on in a whisper, "*Some-kids-are-stealing-stuff-from-your-store.*"

"What's that, dear? Can you speak up a little?"

"It's not ALL of us," Lucy babbled, flinging out her arms to show how many it wasn't.

Her right hand smashed into a counter carousel hung round with little packets of Easter eggs. The display teetered in slow motion. She lunged to steady it, but too late! It toppled forward, raining down bags of speckled pink, yellow, white and green eggs. She staggered backwards, dropping her

47

schoolbag, which dumped its contents all over the floor.

"I'm so sorry—I didn't mean—I'll pick everything up and pay for—." Lucy stared sadly at the packets of eggs she'd stepped on. Why, oh why, did these things always happen to her!

Mrs Collins came round from the back of the counter and picked up the display unit. Lucy knelt down to pick up the scattered bags. "I'm really sorry, I didn't mean –" Lucy repeated.

To Lucy's surprise, Mrs Collins didn't seem angry, just resigned. So, as they gathered up the eggs together, Lucy found she could finally tell her about the shoplifting.

Mrs Collins shook her head sadly, "Oh, I know some children have been trying it on. I haven't caught anyone at it, but I know my stock too well not to notice." She stood up. "Mr Collins has suggested we put up a sign limiting the number of children in the store at any one time." She gave Lucy a tired half smile. "I haven't wanted to, because I like to trust people, kids included."

"Will you put up a sign now?" Lucy asked.

"It looks like I'll have to. Thanks for telling me about the thieving, pity there aren't more like you." She gave Lucy a friendly pat on the shoulder. "Don't worry about the squashed eggs. Here, take an unspoiled packet. On the house."

"Lucy –" a voice called out from behind her.

Suddenly, Lucy remembered Fitzie's face behind the window. What now? She spun round, but it was only Ryan holding out her schoolbag. "I put your books and stuff back inside," he said.

What a surprise! Really nice, Lucy thought.

"Is this yours?" he asked. On his upturned hand lay a Kitkat. He gave her another of those funny looks she'd noticed before.

"No, why?"

"Right." The funny look vanished and he grinned.

Something peculiar is going on, Lucy thought. She returned the Kitkat to the corner display, said goodbye and thanks for the eggs to Mrs Collins. No sign of Fitzie and Alice and the gang when they got outside the shop. No doubt they were round the corner, killing themselves over her egg disaster.

"You go home up the hill, don't you?" she asked Ryan.

Ryan nodded and they set off. He asked, "Do you know where that Kitkat came from?"

"No. Did someone drop it?"

"Someone dropped it all right. Alice! Straight into your bag, when you were looking at cards. I thought you must be part of a complicated plan for nicking sweets." He glanced up at her. He was at least half a head shorter. "I was surprised, because I know they're behind the freeze you're getting at school."

Lucy burst out laughing. "They've been pressurising me to pinch sweets. And I wouldn't. So, they must have thought they'd help me out. Action-Lucy-Shoplift has just been foiled!" She shot her fist in the air. "Yes-s-s-!" Then she frowned. "Foiled, only because I'm so blooming clumsy."

"Well, it was useful," Ryan said.

"For once," Lucy admitted. "Here, have an egg."

Chapter 8

Just when Lucy thought things couldn't get any worse at school, they got *much* worse. The day after the sweet shop business (Buddy had been held up at work and actually apologised), Michelle came back to school. She brought the most devastating news in the whole world! She and her family were moving away, not waiting till the end of the school year, moving *right now!* They'd been house-hunting in a city further north and Michelle hadn't been allowed to tell, in case her dad's new job fell through.

In the remaining two weeks, Lucy and Michelle spent every minute together. There were sleep-overs, a farewell party, and an outing to the pizza cafe. But it was scary how fast the day arrived when Lucy went to school with no Michelle. FOR EVER!

The 'freeze Lucy' campaign, which had thawed during Michelle's final weeks, was on again. Nothing was said. Nothing Lucy could moan to Miss Moan about. It was just that she was completely and totally ignored, in class and especially at break.

One day five teams of two were sent outside for a measuring project. They were allowed to choose a partner. No one chose Lucy, so Miss Moan put

Lucy and Ryan together. Outside, the classroom assistant leant against a wall and kept an eye on them. They were to pace out the playground and school buildings and then draw up a plan to scale.

Pacing the south side of the playground, Lucy and Ryan decided it was 50 metres, near enough.

"I could run it twice and practise the 100 metres," Lucy said.

"Or four times for the 200 metres," Ryan added at once.

"Or eight times for the 400 metres," they both said and laughed. Lucy's first laugh at school for a week. "Should you be talking to me?" she asked.

"I'm not afraid of Fitzie and her mates. I'm not big but I can outrun any of them. Running's my thing."

"I didn't know you were a runner, too," Lucy said, surprised. "I'm hoping to join the Junior Merlins Athletics Club next year, when I go to secondary school."

"*I'm* doing a Fun Run at Brockett Wood this Saturday. Do you know about it? Want to come?" Ryan asked.

"Where's my school skirt?" Lucy shouted down the stairs to her mum on Saturday morning. She had just fed Peep and suddenly remembered the Fun Run.

"In the wash. Why?"

"Oh NO!" cried Lucy. She clattered down the stairs and raced to the washer in the kitchen.

"The leaflet Ryan gave me about the Fun Run is in the pocket of my skirt. It tells the *times and where to meet!*" Lucy's voice rose to a squeak!

"Oh Lucy," her mum sighed. "I must have missed emptying that pocket. The load will be done soon. Maybe it will still be readable."

A few minutes later, Lucy pulled her wet skirt from the washer. In the pocket were tiny sodden bits. It wasn't even recognisable as a leaflet, never mind legible.

"You could phone a friend," Mum said.

"I haven't—that is—" Lucy stopped. She couldn't worry her mum by saying she hadn't got a friend. Anyway, there was Ryan. She could phone him. Ryan Johnson. She rushed to the phone book and stared at the dozens of Johnsons. She didn't know his dad's name. She tried to call up a picture of the leaflet in her head. She seemed to see an 11. Must be an 11 o'clock start.

An hour later at 10.30am, Lucy and her dad set out on the fifteen-minute drive to Brockett Wood. "Hope you're right about this, Miss Muddle," said her dad. "I'm working this afternoon and won't be able to hang around all day, not if you want Brussels sprouts and beetroot on your table," he grinned.

"Yuck and double yuck!" cried Lucy.

They reached the wood, but couldn't find the starting place at once. It had begun to rain and the windscreen kept fogging up. When it was almost 11am, they spotted a yellow banner announcing 'FUN RUN START" and a small group of people in track suits, holding umbrellas.

Dad parked the car and Lucy looked down at her trainers. Yes, laces double-knotted, she'd learnt that lesson. "Bye, Dad, see you later." Lucy leapt out of the car and raced towards the banner.

Ryan pushed out of the group and said, "I thought you weren't coming. Line-up time was 10.30."

Lucy huddled under his umbrella. "Sorry, I, um, trashed the leaflet."

"Quick! Give your name to the organiser." Ryan pointed. "Jeff. The bloke with the black curly hair and green track suit."

Jeff had a clipboard and a whistle round his neck. He looked at Lucy. "One more? It's a wet day and some of the kids have gone home. You OK with rain?"

Lucy nodded and gave her name.

Jeff blew his whistle and made an announcement. "The course is a circuit of two miles. Children can run one circuit, adults can run any number up to five. The whole Fun Run is intended to be 10 miles, but it's filthy weather. So see how it goes."

Ryan and Lucy set off together, running comfortably side by side, most of the adults ahead.

They crossed an open field, jogged down a farm footpath and then entered Brockett Wood. It was an old beech wood with twisty roots in the path, so they had to watch their footing. Lucy's family had picnicked there sometimes in summer. There was an adult leader at the front of the runners and another as a back marker, so there was no way anybody could get lost.

As they came out of the protection of the wood, the rain was tipping down. During a long pull uphill, Lucy and Ryan began to pass some of the puffing grown-ups. The grass was slippery, but they managed to stay upright. After the hill, they splashed down a muddy path. They continued on, not talking much now. Before long, they arrived back at the start of the circuit.

Jeff punched his stop watch and said, "You two have made good time. Especially in this weather. Well done!"

"Can't we go round again?" Lucy begged. She was absolutely drenched, but felt glowing all over and full of strength.

"How old are you?" he asked.

"Almost eleven," she said.

"I *am* eleven," Ryan piped up.

"Sorry. Only one circuit for anyone under 12." He laughed. "Them's the rules. I hadn't realised how young you were. Extra well done, both of you." He wrote something beside their names. Their times, Lucy thought.

"Get home fast, and into dry kit," he advised.

Dad sat reading a newspaper in the car and welcomed Lucy inside. He inspected her.

"You're soaked! Some *Fun* Run! More like, No-Fun Run."

"Definitely No-Sun Run. But I loved it and didn't fall once," said Lucy.

"Wonderful," said Dad, and they went home.

Chapter 9

'Shove up, can't you?" whispered Lucy. It was the day after the Fun Run.

Three kids from her junior youth group shuffled and grumbled and made a tiny gap in the front row at church. Lucy scrunched in, jammed up against the wooden bench end.

"Sorry," mouthed Karen, silently. She sat next to Lucy. Karen rolled her eyes at the family at the other end of the row. They were spread out, with two little kids and a baby in a carry-cot, plus teddies, books, snacks, and a light blanket.

Like they'd come for a picnic, Lucy thought. Well, it was her favourite sort of Sunday, too, when the church youth groups did their stuff. Geena, who Buddy said was drop-dead gorgeous, always played a guitar. Sometimes, but not today, there was a double bass player too. Lucy liked the deep ba-doom it gave to the singing. Then the senior youth group acted out a play from the Bible. The juniors passed the offering baskets. And the infants usually tee-heed through a little song.

To start this Sunday, Geena played two numbers, a jolly one and a slow one, and they watched a play about Jesus curing the sick. Then everybody settled back to listen to the vicar, Mr Cole. Lucy watched as he walked to his speaking stand.

Lucy looked up and he gazed straight down at her.

"Love your enemy!" he said. Lucy gulped and thought of Alice. How could anyone love *her*? Or Fitzie? How could anyone love the gang who'd been so spiteful. How could anyone even *like* any of them? Mr Cole seemed to be reading her mind because he added, "It doesn't mean you have to *like* your enemy."

He told a story about a man who'd risked his life to save his worst enemy from drowning. Afterwards, a newspaper reporter had asked him why: "I heard you didn't even like him."

"The rescuer had replied, 'I don't. But God loves him, so I must too.'"

Mr Cole went on to say that God loves *you,* with all your faults, and even when you do horrible things sometimes. Lucy shrank in her corner. She remembered how cross she'd been with Mini Muddle this morning, how she wouldn't let him help feed Peep.

She glanced up cautiously. Was the vicar looking at her again? It seemed like it, and he was saying, "So if God can find good in you, maybe you can find a good part in the people you thought were your enemies. And love that part."

Did Fitzie and Alice, or any of the gang, have good bits somewhere, Lucy wondered. They must be all shrivelled up, like a raisin.

When Mr Cole had finished, Geena played the guitar again and the infants sang. Lucy and the other junior youth group members collected the offering baskets from the front. The church was big and full, so taking the offering was going to be slow. She and Karen stood at opposite ends of a section of seats and passed a basket back and forth. When the basket was plumped up nicely with envelopes, notes and coins, Lucy glanced at the second to last row. She nearly jumped out of her skin. Talk about enemies, here was one!!

Marcie! The newest member of the gang. Big as life and twice as nasty! For a panicky moment, Lucy feared the whole bunch was lurking there, ready with a new scheme to ruin her life. But when she looked again, a church member she knew sat next to Marcie, and on the other side was a man Lucy hadn't seen before.

Keeping her eyes fixed on her enemy, Lucy took the heaped basket and held it towards old Mrs Trimble at the end of Marcie's row. The old lady's shaky hands reached out, but Lucy let go of the basket too soon.

CRASH! CLATTER! CHING! The noise of coins landing on the polished wood floor was absolutely stunning. The infants faltered and stopped singing. Lucy felt her face burn as a zillion eyes turned her way. She dropped to her knees, scrabbling for coins and apologising. Mrs Trimble tried to totter to her feet to help but was restrained by people nearby. Coins were still rolling away, Lucy saw, as she peered between people's legs. If only she, too, could roll away down a crack in the floor. Then she met a pair of blue eyes down at her level.

"Here's some," offered Marcie, holding out two fistfuls of notes and coins. She dropped them back into the basket. 'You pick up around here. I'll collect money that's scattered."

Lucy knew her mouth was hanging open as

Marcie stood up and moved along the row, collecting.

The infants took up their song again and people faced the front once more. Others dropped handfuls of money back into Lucy's basket. The one who retrieved the most, though, was Marcie. Lucy was completely baffled. What had got into Marcie?

The other three juniors stood at the back, holding their baskets and gesturing at Lucy to hurry up. Finally, she joined them. When they walked to the front of the church, Lucy felt her face must be the colour of a beef tomato. She slunk back to her seat.

After the service was over, she found her mum outside the church. "We were on the other side," she said, "and couldn't see. But Buddy said, 'Bet it's Lucy.' Was it?"

"Trust him," muttered Lucy. "I thought Mrs Trimble had hold of it. She's about a thousand years old and her hands are really trembly." Trimbley, she thought to herself.

"Then why didn't you hold the basket *for* her and pass it to the next person, Lucy, love?" said her mum, "you must concentrate on what you're doing. Otherwise, you'll bounce from one disaster to another."

Lucy hung her head. In the soup again. "Sorry, Mum."

Then she heard a man's voice she didn't know.

"Hello," he said to Mum. He was the one who had been sitting next to Marcie. "I'm Bill Atkins, Marcie's father. I believe your daughter and mine are great friends."

Lucy's jaw dropped. Several paces behind her dad stood Marcie. She looked horrified. She shook her head slightly, as if to say, don't blame me, *I* didn't tell him that.

As Mum turned and shook hands, Lucy realised she'd never mentioned Marcie's name. It was always just Fitzie, Alice and their gang.

Lucy muttered, "Uh, we're in the same class at school."

"So Marcie said when she went to help you pick up the money." He was a tall, smiley man with sandy hair that stuck up at the back. "I'm so pleased to meet one of her friends," he added, as if he really meant it. His voice faded a little. "I live three hours' drive away and only get to see Marcie some weekends. I don't know any of her friends now – or what she gets up to – since she moved here with her mother."

Lucy looked at Marcie. She'd never seen anyone look so embarrassed. Lucy felt almost sorry for her.

"We're going out for pizza for lunch," he continued. "We'd love Lucy to go with us if it's all right with you," he said to Mum. "And you, of course," he said to Lucy. He was taking it for granted that she would be thrilled, she realised.

Marcie didn't say anything. Her usually sleek blonde hair looked ruffled, her green eyes were wide, her hands clenched. How come their parents couldn't see how tense Marcie was, Lucy wondered. So it was up to her. "Mum, Buddy said he'd take me for a timed run this afternoon and he –"

Her mum interrupted, "Oh, well, you can do that afterward." She looked delighted that Lucy had a friend after all. If she only knew – but how could Lucy say, in front of this nice man, that his darling daughter was a bully and a thief?

"We'll drop Lucy back home by two o'clock," Marcie's dad said, "so she'll have time for her run."

Well, as Dad was always saying, every cloud has a silver bin liner. Lucy absolutely adored pizza.

Chapter 10

Lucy took a huge bite of her pizza supremo, loaded with pepperoni, bacon, green peppers, black olives and four kinds of cheese. She was eating quickly so she wouldn't have to make conversation. She also wanted to get this nightmare lunch over as soon as possible. Marcie's dad chatted away, appearing not to notice their stunned silence.

"I take it you're interested in athletics," he said to Lucy, "if you're doing timed runs?"

A safe subject. With relief, Lucy said "I want to be a runner, not sure yet whether a sprinter or a distance runner. I love the long runs, but my brother – he belongs to a club – says I'm probably too tall for distance."

She suddenly thought she had a chance to tell Marcie a few things. "Some of the kids at school call me 'Spaghetti-Legs'."

"Do you like that?" Marcie's dad asked.

"Not much." Lucy shook her head. "I'd rather hear my name. This one girl started calling me that after I beat her in every race at last year's sports day. She's jealous, I suppose, and means it in a nasty way." Lucy glanced over at Marcie. Her face glowed pink.

"Children can be needlessly unkind," Marcie's dad said.

Typical parent remark, Lucy thought, just as if grown-ups were never "needlessly unkind". But he was right about their class, that was for definite.

He stood up and signalled to the waitress. "You girls order ice cream or any sweet you like. I've got to make a phone call. Excuse me for a few minutes."

Lucy and Marcie each disappeared behind a menu. When at last Marcie ordered a Knickerbocker Glory, Lucy said she'd have the same, whatever it was. The waitress took their menus away and returned with two towers of chocolate, strawberry and vanilla ice-cream, topped with chocolate sauce, chopped nuts and a cherry.

Lucy and Marcie faced each other, alone for the first time. Like a cowboy gunfight, Lucy thought. She'd just seen one on TV. Would they splat scoops of ice-cream at each other? She waited.

Finally, the silence got too much.

Lucy said, "Uh, thanks for helping me pick up the money."

Marcie cleared her throat. "And thanks for not telling Dad about, about—"

"About all the dirty tricks you lot are pulling. Is that what you're trying to say?"

"Yeah. I know you must be fed up."

"Too right," Lucy agreed.

"To tell you the truth, I'm getting fed up with it, as well." Marcie pushed her fringe off her forehead. 'I wish I could—"

But Lucy didn't hear what Marcie wished because her dad came back to join them.

Next day in class Lucy kept glancing Marcie's way, but their eyes never met. At break, Lucy lingered in the corridor to give Marcie a chance to speak to her. But she brushed right by with the gang.

"Does anyone smell something funny?" asked Alice, in her smirky voice. Meaning Lucy.

So much for Sunday friendship. Lucy dawdled out into the playground and stood alone under the tree where she and Michelle used to meet.

"Great run on Saturday," a voice said. It was Ryan. "I heard nobody did the full 10 miles. It just got too muddy."

"I wish Jeff had let us do a second round. I wasn't tired a bit."

"Me neither."

Lucy looked him up and down. "You'll get stick talking to me."

"Tough. Anyway, I told you I can outrun 'em," Ryan said. "Look, can you do this?" He sat down on a corner bench, stretched out one leg on it and lowered his upper body onto the leg. He sat up. "Mobility exercise. Dad taught me."

Lucy tried, but could only get part of the way down.

"It took me several months to get down flat. You just have to practise."

Then they did calf muscle and hamstring stretches. The bell rang. The break had whizzed by, like it used to do with Michelle.

But they didn't return to the classroom. The whole school filed into the hall for a special extra assembly. Miss Hadley, the head teacher, stood up in front. She had bright red hair and was so short she could barely see over the reading stand. Usually funny and nice, today she looked grim. Something must be up.

"It has come to my attention," Miss Hadley started, "that pupils from this school have been shoplifting in the local shops."

Lucy slid low in her seat. She'd forgotten her mum was going to ring the school today. Her mum had seen Mrs Collins at the weekend and she was still losing stuff at the sweetshop. Miss Hadley went on, "I visited one of the shops this morning, and from the descriptions I know who some of you are. You have been warned! If I hear of one more incident, I will inform your parents and you'll get detentions every night for the rest of the term. The stealing must stop."

After maths and science, the day was over and Lucy made her way to the cloakroom for her jacket. Fitzie grabbed Lucy's arm and bent it behind her back. "You been snitching, haven't you?"

"I never said a single thing to Miss Hadley," Lucy said truthfully. She wished she had the courage to say, "but my mum did and I'm glad."

"You sure?" Fitzie snarled.

"Yes," Lucy told her.

"Shut it," added Alice, who'd join them. She slashed a finger across her mouth. "We've got new plans for you if you don't. Even your new *boyfriend* won't save you." She said 'boyfriend' with a sneer.

"Huh!" snorted Fitzie. Her broad, freckled face came close to Lucy's. "Ryan, what a shrimp! Is that the best you can do?"

At that moment, Miss Moan looked round the

corner. "What's the noise here? Time you were off home, all of you."

Lucy swiftly picked up her bag, hurried down the steps and out of the school.

The next day she felt tense and uneasy. The gang were going to dump on her again. Something was going to happen today, she just knew it.

Something did happen, but it was nothing to do with the gang.

At the end of the afternoon, the newish teacher from Class 5, Miss Briggs, bounced into the classroom. She was young and sporty, with cropped, streaked blonde hair. Much more fun than Moany, Lucy thought.

Miss Briggs rapped her pencil on Moany's desk and announced, "I'm forming a squad now for the district cross-country meet in six weeks' time. Both Class 5 and 6 are eligible and we need five boys and five girls for the squad."

She waved her clipboard. "Don't be shy. Any number can train, and the runners for the meet will be picked towards the end of training. We'll travel in a coach to the meet and have lunch. It will be lots of fun – and get you fit."

She beamed round the classroom. "First, girl volunteers?"

At the table to her left, Lucy heard Alice muttering, "Who'd want to puff round a field for nothing? Stupid!"

Immediately Lucy stuck up her hand. So did a girl called Zoe and, surprise, surprise, Varsha, one of the gang. Lucy glanced round and saw Alice scowling. Fitzie looked unhappy. She'd wanted to volunteer, Lucy was sure, but old Spaghetti-Legs had got in first. Maybe Fitzie couldn't face Alice's sneers either.

"Any more? Come on, girls," urged Miss Briggs. "Please, I need more girls to volunteer, if we're to have a good squad." Miss Briggs was pleading now.

Very slowly, Marcie put up her hand.

"Good," said Miss Briggs. "That's seven, with the three girls from Class 5. Now the boys.

Five boys including Ryan raised their hands. Miss Briggs took the names and handed out leaflets and letters for parents to sign.

Lucy looked at the leaflet. So much for a happy time in the squad! With TWO of the gang in it, it'll be just like class. Awful!

Chapter 11

Three days later, before school, Lucy and Mini were preparing to feed Peep. He pottered round the garden during the day and swam in Mini's paddling pool. But at night he now slept in a box on the back porch. He was growing fast and had got too big for their bedroom.

Lucy stirred water into wheat and oats to make a wet, crumbly mash while Mini picked some grass. Usually Lucy loved any time spent with Peep, but today other things crowded her mind. Like the gang's doings and today's first cross-country training session.

The gang had stopped the silent treatment. Now they talked *about* Lucy all the time, during break, and whenever they could get away with it in school. Marcie didn't call out any names, but she stuck with the gang.

The worst was Alice. She could think up more nasty stuff than any *normal* person could ever imagine. Lucy answered back once in a while. Mostly she gritted her teeth and kept still. The whole class now knew 'Spaghetti-Legs and Pizza-Feet'. Lucy's feet *were* big, good for running, so there. 'Juicy-Lucy' was the favourite name on the day she had a cold and her nose kept dripping. Others were Stick Insect, Bony-Knees, Skinnybum and Frizzybonce.

Only two things kept her going. First, Ryan was a mate, especially at break. He ignored all the gang's dirty looks and the boys' teasing. Second, her hopes for the cross-country team.

The day crawled by, with the usual ugly stuff from Fitzie, Alice, Sophie and Varsha. But all Lucy's thoughts were on the training to come.

After school the Class 5 and Class 6 squad members, seven girls and eight boys, climbed into track suits and trainers and met Miss Briggs down by the mini-coach.

"We're really lucky," she said. "The local sports shop and one of the supermarkets are funding our coach trips to the park."

They took their seats and set off. Miss Briggs talked as they went. They would be training on Monday, Wednesday, and Friday after school with exercises, jogging, and running. Lucy realised they were going to the park where they'd found Peep. Nearer the meet, continued Miss Briggs, they would practise on real cross-country terrain at Brockett Wood. On the day of the meet, the new coach from Junior Merlins, Mr Lawrence, would be there, selecting new members.

Miss Briggs glanced round the group. "That is, if any of you are interested in joining an athletics club."

At the park she led them through warm-up exercises. Then they began to jog. Lucy would have liked to run faster, but she could hardly run ahead of the teacher. So she paced alongside and told her about her hopes to join Junior Merlins and eventually be an international class athlete. Every ten minutes or so, they walked for a bit to let some of the squad catch their breaths. Lucy looked back from the head of the group. Marcie tailed at the end, with a pink face.

By the third training session, a few days later, they were beginning to work well together.

Miss Briggs had upped the pace and was pleased with them. "We might even be good enough to go on to the All-County Meet." She smiled at the boys. "We've easily got enough boys for the team of five and a sub, and the competition will be hot for those places." Then she nodded at the girls. "We've got excellent runners among the girls too, but not quite enough. Two of you have already told me you don't want to race; you've just come along to get fitter. And that's great. But—?" There was a question in her voice, but she didn't go on.

After the fourth session, Lucy got a shock. When they climbed into the coach, Marcie plonked down next to her.

"Hi," she said. "You can really run."

"Yeah," Lucy said. "What else are Spaghetti-Legs and Pizza-Feet good for?"

Marcie flushed. She took a deep breath as if she'd made a decision. "Do you know why I joined this squad?"

"To run?"

"No. I run like a donkey, as you've noticed, though I'm pleased to get fitter for—well, anyway. I came to make a break from the gang. I don't like their stunts any more. Never did, really. When I saw Fitzie wasn't joining the squad, I thought I could cope with Varsha. She's just a gang hanger-on, like me." Marcie dragged a tissue over her hot-looking face. "I was glad she wasn't at school today, though, because it gives me a chance to talk to you."

Lucy said slowly, "After that day at church, I thought we could – maybe not be friends – but at least not enemies. Then you went right back to the gang."

"I know." Marcie hung her head. "I'm a born coward. I don't know how you stand what they dish out."

"Got no choice." Lucy had an idea suddenly. "If you really want to break with Fitzie and the rest, come and sit with me at lunch tomorrow."

"I'll t-try."

When Lucy went to bed that night, she added an extra to the family round-up of "God bless Mum, Dad, Buddy, Mini and Peep." She prayed, "God bless Marcie, and would you please help her to be brave. She'll be happier away from the gang. And me, I'll be happier, too. I know you're listening, God. So if you could concentrate on Marcie tomorrow, that would be really great."

She snuggled down under the duvet. Then she remembered the way Mum had taught her to finish her prayers. "Not my will, but yours be done. Amen."

Next morning at school, Lucy tried several times to catch Marcie's eye. But she wasn't looking.

At lunch break, Lucy walked quickly into the school hall. Fitzie, Alice, Sophie and Varsha clustered at one end of a table. There was no sign of Marcie. Probably gone home for lunch, coward's way out, Lucy decided. She picked up ham and salad, a roll, fruit yoghurt and apple juice and sat down as far from the gang as possible.

Five minutes passed. Lucy was halfway through her lunch, when Marcie passed down the cafeteria line. She stood with her tray and gazed round the room. The gang waved her over, but she stayed rooted to the spot. Then she squared her shoulders and headed towards Lucy. As always, there was an empty chair beside Lucy.

"Anybody sitting here?" Marcie asked.

"You are, aren't you?"

Marcie crashed down her tray and whooshed out a big breath. "Definitely."

The afternoon was tense. Marcie sat at Alice and Sophie's table in class and they whispered to her non-stop whenever Moany's back was turned. Lucy watched out of the corner of her eye. Marcie nodded and shook her head in turn. Lucy felt sorry for her and sent up a silent prayer, "Please, God, help Marcie stay strong." Lucy was having an easy afternoon with all of the gang's focus on Marcie. Once she caught Ryan's glance and he gave her a quick thumbs up. He must have seen the lunchtime drama.

There was training again after school, two days in a row, because Miss Briggs would be away on Friday. Marcie usually sat with Varsha in the coach, but this time she and Lucy took the front seats together. Varsha looked a bit surprised, but shrugged her shoulders and joined up with a Class 5 girl.

During the training session, Lucy jogged along at the back with Marcie, chatting and encouraging her. Marcie didn't say much. She needed to save her breath.

At teatime that night, while the family hoovered up their macaroni cheese, Lucy said, 'I think I've got a new friend – and you'll never guess who."

"WHO?" they chorused. Except Buddy. "Is it a creature from Outer Space, who doesn't know any better?" he asked.

Lucy gave him a swift kick under the table, and said, "Nope, not Outer Space. From Inner Gang." She grinned at him. "It's happened because I'm such a wonderful and forgiving person." She looked at her dad. "And I prayed too like you said – to be calm and stand my ground, but never do anything their way."

Then she told them about her day.

Chapter 12

A week later, Miss Briggs announced, "We're going to start cross-country training at Brockett Wood on the Wednesday sessions. That'll be much more fun than chugging round the park." She glanced at her clipboard. "And I'm still looking for at least one more good girl runner. But she needs to join now or it'll be too late in the training. Any ideas, talk to me on the journey home."

During some training sessions Lucy steamed away at the front of the group with Ryan and Miss Briggs. Today, however, she dawdled at the back with her friend Marcie, who really was moving better now.

"You know who's a good runner?" Lucy said to Marcie.

"No, who?"

"Fitzie. Remember, I said I beat her in every race last sports day. Only *just* beat her in some, and she was second every time."

"Oh no, you don't!" Marcie looked panicky. She'd had a bad time with the gang. Alice had been furious and nasty. "Mousey," they called her now, and pretended she squeaked and ran up kids' legs. Alice had rubbed a mouldy bit of cheese into her English homework.

Lucy tried another tack. "Look, together we can

stand up to Fitzie. Bringing her in will be for the good of the school and the squad. Maybe we could even *win* the meet!"

Marcie looked unconvinced. Lucy tried harder. "Haven't you seen her watch us get on the coach? She'd love to come if it weren't for Alice. Without Alice she might be all right."

"Doubt it," Marcie panted, as they returned to the coach. Five minutes of warm-down exercises later and she said, "Oh all right."

"How come you joined Fitzie's gang anyway? You sound like you *never* liked them much." Lucy was puzzled.

"On my first day at school, Alice said 'Come and sit with us' at lunchtime. Nobody else did. You and Michelle never asked me to be with you."

This was true. They hadn't been unfriendly. But they hadn't gone out of their way to be nice, either. "Yeah, right," Lucy said. Message received.

On the ride back to school, Lucy told Miss Briggs about Fitzie, and how her best friend wouldn't want her to join so she'd probably need persuading. Miss Briggs smiled and said, "Leave it to me."

The very next training session, just as the coach door was about to shut, Fitzie climbed inside. She wasn't swaggering now. She bit her lip and didn't know where to sit. Lucy thought, she's the outsider now. Now she knows how it feels. Then Varsha called out, "There's a place by me, Fitzie."

Marcie and Lucy were in the back row and Lucy glanced out of the window. Alice was standing on the corner, her fists clenched, her mouth twisted into a snarl. Lucy shivered, in spite of herself.

The days passed and Lucy didn't mind going to

school now. She and Marcie hung out together, with Ryan part of the time. The squad members often sat together at lunch break and discussed their chances of placing and going on to the All-County Meet. Fitzie and Varsha, however, stayed with Alice and Sophie at lunchtimes. Lucy noticed Alice forever dragging Fitzie into corners and talking earnestly. Lucy thought she was trying desperately to keep control of the gang.

On Monday afternoon, during Art, Alice raised her hand and asked to go to the toilet.

"It's the last lesson. Can't you wait?" demanded Moany.

"No, I can't." Alice pulled her pointy face into a smirk.

"All right then."

Five minutes later, Lucy realised she needed to go too. Too much apple juice at lunch. Plus an extra glass of water. Briggsy was always telling them to drink plenty of water to prevent dehydration.

Lucy waited for Alice to come back. Moany allowed only one out at a time. Finally she couldn't last any longer and asked permission.

"Where has Alice got to?" Miss Moan enquired of the class. "Go on, then, Lucy, and tell her to come back right now," she ordered.

Lucy started through the cloakroom toward the girls' toilet when something moved. What? She stopped and stared into the dim corner by the radiator. It was Alice. She was on her knees, a row of little yellow-topped containers beside her. In front of her was Lucy's blue sports bag, zipped open. She knew it by the orange tag.

"WHA'D'YA THINK YOU'RE DOING?" cried

Lucy, rushing forward.

Alice jumped up and tried to kick the yellow things behind a fallen coat.

Then Lucy saw that her trainers were out of the bag. One of the yellow things was stuck on the back of a trainer where Alice had dropped it. Lucy grabbed up the trainer and shrieked. The yellow thing was a plastic pot of honey, the kind served with toast in motorway cafes. It was dripping honey all down the outside of her trainer. The other honey pots had their lids opened too, ready to be glopped, Lucy knew it, *inside* her trainers! Ready to ruin them and her chances in the cross-country!

Lucy grabbed Alice's hand and hung on. She couldn't speak, she was so angry. Alice's hand was sticky and so, now, was Lucy's.

Alice squeaked and tried to wrench herself free.

"What do you two think you're doing?" shouted Moany who must have heard the noise.

"What muddle is this, Lucy?"

Lucy and Alice stood holding hands, stuck together.

"Er, we're having an argument," said Lucy. She tore her hand off Alice's.

Moany was not pleased and gave them both a detention. The worst of it was missing training, but at least it wasn't a Brockett Wood day. After school, Lucy and Alice copied out a nine-line poem ten times. Ninety lines altogether. The poem was about a rainbow and about a child being the father of a man, whatever that meant. Stretching out her cramped fingers, Lucy looked over at Alice, who was scribbling away furiously, and wondered what made her so foul.

Later, when Lucy told Buddy about the honey pot plot, he ruffled her hair and said, "Poor old Lucy. Sorry for your troubles. Get Miss Briggs to keep your sports kit." He examined her sticky trainer. Lucy thought his face looked angry. "That Alice is a menace!" he muttered.

As he finished cleaning up her trainer, he said, "Remember, I promised I'd speak to the Junior Merlins coach about you?" he asked. As if she needed reminding! "Just found out my mate's left. I don't know the new one."

"That's OK. Briggsy told us the new coach will be at the district cross-country meet."

Buddy gave her a thumbs-up. "Better run your socks off then." And before tea, he took her for a jog in the park, to make up for the lost session.

"We'll give Peep a treat and let him swim in the pond while we run."

"What if he won't come back?" cried Lucy.

"Then he's ready to go back to the wild."

Lucy gasped. She wasn't ready to give Peep up yet.

They set Peep down at the edge of the pond. He lifted his beak, his beady eyes fixed on them, asking, Lucy thought, aren't you coming in too? She giggled, remembering how she'd joined him in the bath.

Buddy gave Peep a nudge toward the water. "Go and say 'hello' to all those nice duckies over there."

Peep didn't look at all convinced that those duckies were nice. He stepped carefully alongside the pond for a little while. Finally, he tiptoed in and began to swim away from them.

After the run, they found Peep paddling by himself at one end of the pond. Maybe the other ducks had been unfriendly. Lucy knew what that felt like.

"Come on Peep, let's go home," Lucy called. He gave a little sound. More of a quack now than a peep and swam over.

"He still wants to live with us," Lucy said happily.

Lucy told no one but Marcie about Alice's honey horror. Marcie shook her head and said, "She's the pits. Funny, Fitzie's all right when we train. No 'Mousey' or 'Spaghetti-Legs'."

Lucy nodded. "Alice is the ringleader. When she's not around—" Lucy didn't finish. She didn't need to.

On Wednesday, during the harder run in Brockett Wood, Fitzie and Miss Briggs were up at the front, running side by side, with Lucy and Ryan just behind.

Lucy heard Miss Briggs say to Fitzie, 'You've got real potential as a runner, Sarah. I'm so pleased Lucy told me about you."

Fitzie shot a shocked look over her shoulder at Lucy. Fitzie's eyes grew even bigger when Lucy smiled at her. Lucy knew she was thinking "what's going on?"

Chapter 13

After the Brockett Wood run, during the warm-down exercises, Fitzie stood beside Lucy. She rested her hands on her bent left leg and stretched out the right one, her big, freckled face puzzled. "How come you wanted me to join the squad?"

"Simple. We needed you," Lucy said. "You and I are the best runners in the class."

"But—" Fitzie began. Hanging in the air between them were all the names and niggly, hateful things that had happened.

"The squad's a new start," Lucy said. "OK?"

"OK," Fitzie said.

With homework and training, trips to the park for Peep and babysitting Mini Muddle for extra pocket money, Lucy put Alice right out of her mind. Then, one day, after a rocket from Moany about Lucy dripping ketchup on her maths homework, she came out of school late and walked smack into a noisy row.

Alice was shouting at a big man in a T-shirt. His fat belly hung over his belt.

"No, I won't!" she cried.

"You'll do as I say, you little—." The man dropped his voice and Lucy couldn't hear what he called Alice.

"GET IN!" he roared, pointing at a dusty black car.

"NO!"

The man suddenly slapped Alice hard on the side of her head. Her knees buckled. He scooped her up and threw her on the back seat, and they drove away.

Lucy took a shaky breath and said out loud, "Poor Alice."

When she told Marcie next day, Marcie nodded. "Fitzie says Alice doesn't get on with her stepdad. He's on the road most of the time, a rep or lorry driver or something like that. When he's home, there's trouble." Marcie shrugged. "She probably winds him up. You know what she's like."

"He swatted her like she was a fly," Lucy protested. "No kid deserves that." Not even Alice, she thought. The travelling stepdad explained the supply of motorway honey pots.

Maybe he also helped make Malice Alice the way she was. Maybe she took out on everybody else the way she felt about him.

Lucy decided she would talk to Dad about it. Her lovely, jokey dad – maybe she didn't appreciate him enough. Lucy thought a quick prayer in her head. "Thank you, God, for my dad. And please make me remember Alice's stepdad when I feel like hating her. She's really hard to be nice to, so I'll need your help. Oh, and *she* really, really needs your help."

The following Sunday was "Goodbye-to-Peep-Day." Lucy had begged to keep him longer, but Peep now paddled happily with the other ducks during his visits to the pond. His head was going greeny-blue, like a grown-up duck. Lucy invited Marcie to come to the farewell and for lunch after.

First, they all went to church. Lucy remembered how the vicar had said, "Love your enemy" all those weeks ago. No good bits in the gang, she'd thought. Not true. She glanced at Marcie, her ex-enemy.

When they knelt for prayers, Lucy whispered, "Thank you, God, for my new friend. I want her to come here with me every Sunday, only her mum won't usually let her. Can you help with that, please?"

When the offering basket went by, Lucy wondered whether Marcie remembered that other Sunday. It turned out she did. She said to Lucy in a low voice "Hey, should I throw my money on the floor?"

Lucy dug Marcie in the ribs and swallowed her giggles.

The farewell to Peep didn't take long. All the family and Marcie stood beside the pond. Lucy and Mini Muddle held Peep together and lowered him into the water.

"GOODBYE, PEEP" they all cried. Buddy dug into his pocket and threw up a handful of confetti.

"He's not getting married," Lucy protested.

"You don't know," said Buddy and pointed. Peep was swimming briskly toward the other ducks.

All of a sudden, it was the last day before the cross-country meet. Miss Briggs took the squad through a light training session on the final Friday. They worked through lots of stretch and mobility exercises, a bit of jogging, but not a long run.

The boys' team was: Ryan, Steve, Kevin, Ali and a Class 5 boy, plus another Class 5 boy as a sub. The girls' team was: Lucy, Fitzie, Varsha, Zoe, with two Class 5 girls as the final member and sub. The remaining Class 5 children who hadn't been picked had another chance next year.

"Are you sure, now, Marcie, you don't want to come along, even as a sub?" Miss Briggs asked. "You've made tremendous progress."

Marcie shook her head. "I'll come as cheerleader. I only wanted to keep fit for ice-skating."

ICE-SKATING!! Lucy realised there was a lot still to know about her new friend.

Miss Briggs handed out information sheets. "Remember, the mini-coach leaves for Northland Country Park from the coach depot on Marshall Street, NOT the school, at 9.30am sharp! Don't be late. We want to be in plenty of time for warm-up."

When Lucy got home, she checked her kit for the second time. Yes, best red track suit, white vest and blue running shorts were neatly folded and ready. She cleaned her trainers and put a new lace in one. She put a water bottle and towel in her bag, plus an anorak in case it rained and suntan cream in case the sun was boiling. She reminded Buddy that he was taking her to the depot at 9am.

"It's only fifteen minutes away," he protested.

"I want to be in plenty of time."

She'd asked Mum for a special meal. She ate a huge lean beefburger. High protein, like Miss Briggs said. With carrots and salad and a glass of milk.

"No chips for runners?" asked Dad as he forked up Lucy's favourite food.

"No chips for run-ners," sang Mini Muddle, swirling his chip round a puddle of ketchup.

"Don't rub it in, you miseries. I've got to be at peak strength tomorrow."

"You're really organised," Mum said admiringly.

"Everything's got to go right. If we make one of the top two places, Briggsy says we'll go to the All-County Meet. Get to stay overnight in a motel. Eat out, stuff like that." Lucy took a bite of carrot. "But the most important thing is to impress the Junior Merlins coach."

"You'll do it," said Buddy. He gave her a thumbs up. For once he didn't add a smart crack about muddles.

Lucy set her alarm for 7.30am, climbed under her duvet an hour early and said her prayers. She added, "Please God, don't let anything go wrong tomorrow." She was all prepared for a great day. She'd thought of everything.

Next morning, Lucy carried on with her written-out schedule. Shower, followed by a healthy break-fast. She tucked into a bowl of muesli with yoghurt and sliced banana on top, followed by a soft-boiled egg and toast soldiers. She packed two high-energy cereal bars in her bag. She unscrewed the bottom of her piggybank and took out £3 emergency money.

Dad was off to work. A weekend shift meant extra money they needed. He gave Lucy a huge smacker on the cheek and said, "Knock 'em dead, kid. Shall I start saving to go to the next Olympics?"

"Absolutely," Lucy said.

Mum was doing a morning at the cash'n'carry. She hitched on her shoulder bag and said, "Mini's all ready to go with you. He's doing a puzzle up in your bedroom." She gave Lucy a hug. "I'm so proud of the way you prepared for this. Good luck!" She rushed out of the door to catch the bus.

At 8.45am Lucy said to Buddy, who was reading the sports page, "Let's go."

Without looking up, he answered, "Not till 9 o'clock. Otherwise, you'll be hanging around by yourself at the coach depot."

Lucy began to pace up and down. She was so excited. She couldn't think of anything else to do.

After a little while, Buddy threw down the newspaper and grinned. "Oh, all right. I can't stand the tension. I'll just give Mini a shout and we'll go." He went to the bottom of the stairs. "C'mon down, Mini. Let's take Lucy for her big race. Hurry up!"

Then he went to the cupboard and pulled out Mini's jacket.

Lucy picked up her sports bag and waited.

"I'm hopping down," called Mini. "I'm a bunny."

She heard thud, thud, thumpety, thumpety. A piercing scream.

BUMP, CRASH, BANG!

Chapter 14

Lucy flung down her bag and raced to the bottom of the stairs, Buddy right behind. Mini lay in a crumpled heap, his face white as paper.

"OHHHH! MINI, ARE YOU ALL RIGHT?"

His eyes fluttered open. He sat up and began to cry huge, shuddering sobs. Buddy knelt and gently felt Mini's legs. He lifted the right arm.

When Buddy touched the left arm, Mini shrank away and cried out: "OW! OW!"

"It might be broken," Buddy muttered to Lucy. "Sprained at the very least. Stupid, stupid stairs with no carpet." He felt all round Mini's little body, but nothing seemed to hurt but the arm. Buddy made a sort of chair of his own arms and Lucy helped Mini into it.

"I'll need to get him straight to A&E, Lucy. The bus depot's the wrong direction or I'd take you on the way. I'm sorry about your race."

THE RACE! She'd forgotten. Just for a moment. Her heart dropped to her toes.

Buddy went on. "If you can't get a neighbour to give you a lift, call a taxi. The number's stuck on the fridge. Dig in my back, left pocket for my wallet. Take out a fiver."

Lucy kissed Mini on the cheek and said to him, "It'll be all right, little Mini. Buddy will take good care of you."

She opened the front door, then the car door. Buddy settled Mini inside and covered him with a blanket. "Good luck!" he said and drove away.

"It's not fair. It's not fair." Lucy blinked back the tears. Then she felt selfish, worrying about a race when her little brother was hurt and in pain.

She phoned Marcie. It rang and rang and then she got the ansaphone. They must have gone already. She raced across the street to the Martins. They were kind and friendly. But nobody answered the bell. Lucy glanced at her watch. It was 9.10. No time to waste. She pelted back home and tore the taxi card off the fridge. She stabbed at the numbers on the phone. Her hand shook.

"Taxis," said a voice.

"Can you send a cab right away to – " Lucy started to give her address.

"Just a minute," the voice interrupted. "Nobody's free for 30–40 minutes. We've got two drivers off sick."

"*That's too late!*" wailed Lucy and put down the phone. Granny George two doors down. She'd try her.

"Come in, Lucy. What's the trouble? You look all hot and bothered. Would you like a cup of tea?"

Lucy panted out her story and begged for a lift to the coach depot. "Of course, my dear," Granny said. But Granny took ages. First, Lucy had to hunt for her spectacles. Then they both searched for her car keys. Next she changed her shoes. Finally she had to telephone her sister not to come over till later. Agony! The minutes whizzed by. At last they were in the car and eventually pulled in alongside the coach depot. There was no mini-coach in sight. Lucy rushed into the office. The coach had left fifteen minutes ago!

Lucy tried hard to keep her voice steady as she told Granny. The old lady patted Lucy's shoulder and said she'd take Lucy to Northland Country Park. "It's a nice day. It'll make a pleasant drive."

Lucy tried to reckon her chances. The mini-coach had had an early start. Briggsy had planned plenty of time for warm-up. Lucy might just make it if only Granny would drive faster. Lucy clenched her fists and gritted her teeth, trying with sheer force of will to hurry her. She leant sideways to see the speedometer. It was 34 mph. Lucy groaned inside, but how could she say anything when Granny was being so kind? The old lady clutched the wheel and stared straight ahead. She'd put on a blue hat with a yellow flower that quivered a little. She was probably nervous. Maybe she hardly ever drove out of town. "Please, please, God, let her drive faster," Lucy prayed.

Why, oh why, hadn't the Martins' son been home? Speedo Martin. He roared up in his banger, with tyres screeching and radio blaring. He'd have got her to the race in time. Lucy tried to relax and stretch her legs, wriggle her toes, uncurl her fingers. She wouldn't be able to run at all if she arrived all tense.

At last, at last they reached the country park. Granny dawdled down the winding road to the car park. Lucy could see a crowd of people milling about nearby and a big, red race banner.

Before Granny had quite stopped the car, Lucy was out of it, babbling. "Thanks a million, Granny

George, no need to wait, I'll come back on the coach, tell you about it tomorrow." She pelted towards the banner. Maybe she was in time.

But there were no junior kids waiting to run. Only secondary kids for the next, longer race. And parent-types laughing and joking. Drinking cans of coke. Also some little kids trying pretend races.

SHE WAS TOO LATE!

Out of the corner of her eye she saw Miss Briggs with her back turned, talking to somebody in a track suit. Lucy wasn't ready to face her yet.

She jogged away from the crowd, digging her fists in her eyes, sniffing back hot tears. No chance to do well in the race. No chance to impress the Junior Merlins coach. She'd let Briggsy, her school and all her team-mates down, her plans and training all for nothing. It wasn't fair.

She tracked along a high hedge for a few hundred meters and then turned back toward the crowd. She took a deep breath. If her team did well, she'd have to be happy for them. She suddenly thought of Marcie. The cheerleader. She'd go and tell her the sad story.

She wandered through the crowd but couldn't find Marcie. Maybe she was ill. Stop putting it off, she scolded herself. Time to see Miss Briggs. What a rocket she'd get!

She dreaded it.

Lucy found Miss Briggs near the race finish line about fifty metres from the starting place. She was chatting with another man in a track suit and turned when Lucy touched her on the arm.

"Uh, Miss Briggs, I'm so sorry—"

Chapter 15

"LUCY! Where WERE you?" cried Miss Briggs. "I tried to contact you on my mobile. Then we took the mini-coach by your house on the way out of town."

"OH NO!" Lucy cried. "I was at the neighbours trying to get a lift." Then she told her story and waited for the bomb to drop.

But Miss Briggs looked concerned, not cross. "Lucy, how terrible! You must have been so worried about your little brother. Thank you for making such an effort to get here." She grinned, suddenly. "Guess who's running in your place!"

"Who?!"

"Marcie. Our Class 5 sub has flu, so when you didn't come, we all leaned on Marcie to run. I shouldn't think we'll place without you, but – " Miss Briggs shrugged – "these things happen." She looked at her watch. "They should start coming round that corner in about a minute. Why don't you go and meet them, and encourage our lot over those last tired uphill metres."

Lucy dropped her bag by Miss Briggs. She stretched out her legs and loped down beside the trail. How good it felt to run at last, even a little way. She checked over the rules in her mind. With five runners, each one counted. It was the position of the whole team that was important. No good having first and second and all the rest coming in at the back.

HERE THEY CAME! But where were her teammates? OH THERE! Fitzie was fourth, plugging uphill looking tired. Lucy sprinted down and waited by the track.

"COME *ON*, FITZIE! YOU CAN DO IT! PASS THE ONE AHEAD!"

Fitzie gave her a startled look and put on a little burst of speed. She overtook the girl in front. Looking up towards the finish line, Lucy saw her come in third.

Next, Lucy cheered in Zoe and Varsha, who were running together. They raced each other to the finish for sixth and seventh places. The Class 5 girl heard Lucy's yell and managed to hang on to her tenth place. But where was Marcie? What if she gave up halfway? She said she ran like a donkey. NO! Here she was, in the middle of a whole bunch of runners.

Lucy ran alongside her and said, "GO, MARCIE GO!" Red-faced and panting, Marcie came in at nineteenth. That wouldn't be good enough for the team to place, Lucy was sure.

But Miss Briggs looked pleased. "Brilliant!" she cried. She raised her stopwatch. "You all ran personal best times and this is a tougher course than we've trained on. Well done!"

Then they went to cheer in the boys, who had set off fifteen minutes after the girls. Ryan was second and the others close behind.

Lucy told her morning's story over and over again as the runners came in. They waited tensely.

The race organiser was tapping his microphone, blowing into it and saying, "Testing, testing."

After a bit of waffle, he got to the point. Linklawn Girls School first. Bremner girls TIED FOR SECOND with Southwing, so THREE teams will go to the All-County Meet! Lucy grabbed Marcie and they jumped round and round. Fitzie and the others joined in and they hugged and danced till they all fell in a heap. Then it happened all over again when Bremner boys got FIRST!

"SSSSHHHHHH!" Briggsy was trying to be heard. "I've brought a picnic lunch to share before we go home. While we set out the stuff, will Ryan, Ali, Steve, Fitzie and Lucy go and have a word with Mr Lawrence?" She waved her arm. "The chap in the green track suit with the clipboard."

Lucy's heart started to thump. MR LAWRENCE! The Junior Merlins coach. She looked all round, but couldn't see anybody in a green track suit except—

"BUT YOU'RE JEFF!" she blurted out as they came up to him. "From the Fun Run."

He grinned, "That's right, Jeff Lawrence. And *you're* Lucy from the Fun Run."

She hung her head. "But I didn't get to run today."

"I heard about it from your teacher. Don't worry," he tapped his clipboard. "I had you on my list already. You were so keen on that foul rainy day. Keenness combined with ability is exactly what I'm looking for."

He spread out his arms to include the others. "I hope all five of you will think about joining Junior Merlins, starting this summer. If you're interested, give me your full names and phone numbers and I'll be in touch with more info."

The teams were ravenous, including Lucy. It was not due to exercise, in Lucy's case, but relief and JOY! They wolfed down ham and cheese brown rolls, celery strips, bananas, muesli bars, and apple juice. No junk food from Briggsy.

"Are you going to take up running?" Lucy teased Marcie.

"What? The donkey derby?"

"You were blooming brilliant for a donkey," Lucy said.

"It's the donkey's first and last race! *You* will be the one running for All-County. Me for cheerleader. OK?"

"OK!" said Lucy.

Just then she heard her name being shouted. She swivelled round to see Buddy and Mini.

"See my arm!" cried Mini waving his plaster cast. His fingers wiggled at the end of it. "It's broked," he added, proudly.

"What a beautiful plaster!" Lucy hugged him. 'What a brave boy!"

"It's only a green-stick fracture," Buddy said, "you know, not broken all the way through. It will heal fine, the doctor said. What happened about the race?"

Beaming, Lucy began to tell the story.

Some more books to enjoy!

Lion Hunt
Ruth Kirtley

High time, short point at four.
Climb a lofty guardian;
What stops his roar?

Will Ashley and Rachel be able to work out the clues in time? And will the clues lead them to something that will save the house from being taken over by the scheming Mr Doubleby?

For Ashley especially, there is much more to this than a hunt for hidden loot.

ISBN 1 85999 412 1
Price £3.99

Available from your local Christian bookshop

Where Dolphins race with Rainbows
Jean Cullop

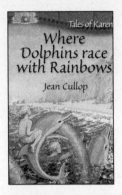

"Welcome to Karensa!"

Luke opened his eyes, blinking in the strong
sunlight. He was sprawled on his back on soft
dry sand. In front of him the sea was calm and
deepest blue.

So the mist and the storm were a dream? But as
he struggled to sit up he realised that there had
been no dream. This was not Poldawn. And he
was being watched by a group of the strangest
people he had ever seen.

What is this strange land to which the dolphins
have brought Luke and Rosie?

ISBN 1 85999 383 4
Price £3.50

Available from your local Christian bookshop

Castle of Shadows
Jean Cullop

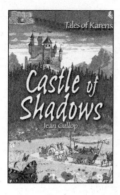

The story begun in *Where Dolphins race with Rainbows* continues with another exciting adventure.

As the cart clattered across the bridge into the courtyard Morwen reminded herself that she had promised not to go inside the castle. She would only look inside the door and then slip away. But to her horror, the iron portcullis dropped down behind them and a chill of fear grippped her heart. She stumbled and a hand took hers. She looked up and found herself staring at Lord Bellum.

"You see, I was right," he said softly. "Did I not say that one day you would walk into my castle of your own free will?"

ISBN 1 85999 463 6
Price £3.50

Available from your local Christian bookshop

Flood Alert!
Kathy Lee

It was stupid, I know that now. But there was no time to think. Helpless as a bit of straw, I was tossed and shaken and dragged under water. I fought my way up – then before I could snatch a breath I went under again.

"Help!" I shouted.

"Don't bother," said Kerry. "They won't hear."

I was sinking, I was going down for the last time...

ISBN 1 85999 301 X
Price £3.99

Available from your local Christian bookshop